Rocco

Danger Bluff, Book One

Becca Jameson

Pepper North

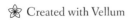 Created with Vellum

About the Book

Welcome to Danger Bluff where a mysterious billionaire brings together a hand-selected team of men at an abandoned resort in New Zealand. They each owe him a marker. And they all have something in common–a dominant shared code to nurture and protect. They will repay their debts one by one, finding love along the way.

Rocco

A mysterious billionaire saved my life.
Now, I owe him.
My team's job: Save Sadie at all costs.
My goal: Convince her she's mine.

Sadie

I wish I'd never noticed that error.
Now, I'm jobless, homeless, and broke.
Thank goodness the resort at Danger Bluff is hiring.
If only that chiseled mountaineer didn't ooze Daddy vibes.

Prologue

"You have two choices. Jump, or I'll shoot you in the head. Either way, you're going off this cliff."

Rocco held up both hands. "You don't have to do this, man. I'm nobody—a mountain guide. I got your men through the pass. Just take the rest of the provisions and leave me here. I don't care what you and your men have done or what you intend to do. I saw nothing." He prayed he could reason with these assholes, but that didn't seem likely.

Rocco was fucked. He glanced behind him. He was less than two feet from the ledge. If he jumped, he would die on impact.

Janks, the bearded stout man who was the ringleader of this organization, laughed sardonically. "You know too much, motherfucker. Which is it going to be? You jump, or I shoot? Personally, I think getting shot between the eyes is the better option. Slightly quicker death than pissing yourself while you fall into the ravine. Either way, it doesn't matter. No one will ever find your body."

Rocco knew Janks was right. No one would even be

1

looking for Rocco. He was a one-man gig. A nomad who spent his life in the mountains. His current source of income was guiding people through the mountain pass. Looked like he'd picked the wrong group this time.

Rocco had had suspicions about this group from the beginning, over a week ago. But last night had been the clincher. He'd overheard the men discussing what they were going to do with their money after this massive drug run. He doubted they'd ever intended to let him live anyway, but when they'd seen him standing at the edge of the campsite, they'd lost their shit, grabbed him, and tied him to a tree for the night.

They'd needed him for one more day. They hadn't known the route. They never would have survived and exited the mountain pass without him.

Rocco had spent the day trying to figure out what the fuck to do to get out of this situation, and he'd come up blank. He'd had a gun, but it was now in the possession of the drug smugglers.

"Three seconds, asshole," Janks growled, cocking the gun.

Suddenly, a shot rang out. Janks dropped to the ground. The other five smugglers turned around and rushed toward their comrade.

"What the fuck?" one of them shouted, advancing on Rocco.

Rocco was just as astounded as they were. He certainly hadn't shot Janks.

Another shot pierced the air, and then four more. In seconds, all six men were dead.

Rocco lowered his arms and staggered forward to put some distance between himself and the cliff's edge. He was lucky he hadn't stumbled backward in the mayhem and fallen to his death after all.

Rocco

He dropped to the ground a second later. Whoever had just shot these six drug smugglers probably wanted the drugs. They would think Rocco was one of them.

Four masked men wearing all black stepped out of hiding, all of them coming toward Rocco, who rolled over onto his back and held up his hands in surrender. "I'm not with them."

One of the men came directly to him and offered a hand as if to help him to his feet. "We know. Rocco Thompson?"

Rocco swallowed as he took the offered hand and rose. "Yes. Who are you?"

"That doesn't matter. What matters is that we know who *you* are." The man nodded toward his three companions as they each dragged two of the fallen men to the edge of the cliff and kicked them over the precipice. They launched their gear over after them.

It all took less than fifteen seconds and left Rocco stunned and confused. He had no idea if he was safe or next on the list to die and get tossed over the edge.

The man beside him reached into his pocket and pulled out a strange gold coin. He held it out.

Rocco opened his hand and caught the coin as his rescuer dropped it into his palm. It wasn't currency. It had no markings on it except for a swirl etched into the face. "What's this?" he asked, lifting his gaze.

"A marker. Your benefactor will collect when he's ready. You owe him one." Then, he and his companions turned and left—so fast Rocco had no chance to respond or ask questions. He was left standing on the edge of a cliff in the middle of nowhere, holding the strangest gold coin he'd ever seen.

A marker? What the fuck? What would he owe someone who'd saved him?

3

Chapter One

Two years later...

Rocco stepped out of the SUV he'd rented, grabbed his duffle from the back seat, and turned to stare up at the front of the Danger Bluff Mountain Resort. The structure was old and in some disrepair, but that didn't surprise him.

Rocco had done quite a bit of research about this place since receiving the certified letter summoning him last week. The letter had the same gold-swirled emblem on both the outside and the inside. It was the first time he'd seen the resemblance since its likeness had been placed in his palm two years ago.

The letter had instructed him to be at this resort in New Zealand at noon today. Considering the mysterious bene-factor who'd saved his life two years ago had indeed kept Rocco's ticker ticking, Rocco had felt compelled to comply with the request. Or perhaps he'd simply been curious. *Besides*, he'd told himself, *what else do I have going on?*

What Rocco knew was that this resort had shut down about a year ago. The owners had run out of funds to keep it operating. It consisted of this main building and a dozen cabins in the surrounding hills. It wasn't currently open for business while it underwent repairs and renovations.

Taking a deep breath, Rocco shrugged his duffle higher on his shoulder and climbed the stairs leading up to the wrap-around porch. For a moment, he considered knocking, but that seemed ridiculous. It wasn't a residence. So, he opened the front door and stepped inside.

The large entryway was empty and kind of dusty. The only piece of furniture—if you could call it that—was a huge wooden reception desk. Behind it was an old-fashioned hotel room key board. It looked like all the keys were still on it.

Rocco found himself shuffling in that direction. Were those keys still useful? Surely not. Hell, he didn't even know if this resort was still a resort. He had no idea why he was here or who he might be meeting. Even though he'd read that the resort closed last year, he'd seen no indication someone had purchased it. It was not, however, listed as an available real estate property.

A movement to the left of the hanging keys caught his eye, and he shifted his attention in that direction as a woman pushed through a swinging door, emerging behind the reception desk.

"Oh," she exclaimed, "you must be Rocco." She smiled at him and then blew a lock of hair off her forehead before reaching up with both hands to tug her ponytail holder free, gather her long messy brown hair together, and reposition the band.

The act mesmerized him. Something about her stirred his nurturing side—a side he hadn't indulged in for far too long.

How long had it been since he'd even entertained the idea of Daddying a Little girl?

As he watched this petite woman mess with her hair, he found himself wanting to round the counter, brush her hands aside, and fix it himself. He wanted to run his fingers through the length over and over until he had it all gathered on top of her head.

As she finished fussing with it, she lifted her brows. "You are Rocco, right?"

Oh shit. He hadn't answered her. "Yes."

"I'm Sadie."

"Are you the one who summoned me?"

She giggled, the noise heading straight for his heart. Or maybe it was his groin. Both. "Heavens no. I'm the new reception manager. I was just instructed to show all of you to the conference room."

Rocco lifted a brow. "All of who?"

She shrugged as she rounded the counter. "The other five men. You're the last to arrive."

Other five men... Interesting.

"Who are we meeting with?"

She shrugged again. "I have no idea."

He frowned. This was weird. Like *The Twilight Zone* weird. He half expected this place to be haunted. Which was absurd.

"Do those keys work?" he asked, pointing at the hanging display. For some reason, that felt like an important question.

"I don't think so. I think the previous owners just left them there to create an ambiance of days gone by. There are coded keycards in the back room for the cabins and the rooms in this main building."

"Ahh." That told Rocco a lot about the resort. It maintained an old-world look but had modern conveniences.

Good to know. "So, I guess the cabins have running water and electricity," he teased.

She giggled again. "Yes." Her ponytail hung over one shoulder, and she twirled it around a finger. Now that she'd emerged from behind the counter, he could take in the rest of her.

She was about five-five and thirty years old, he guessed, nice figure, shapely. She wore a navy sundress with a full skirt that hung almost to her knees and gold sandals. It was a warm day.

Rocco found himself oddly drawn to this woman, and the attraction was growing by the moment. Her dimples were adorable, and every time she licked her full lips, he wanted to taste them, too.

Maybe he'd been out of the scene for so long that the first woman he set eyes on caught his attention, but Rocco thought it was more than that. The attraction was instantaneous and not waning.

"Is the resort reopening?"

She nodded, her ponytail flipping over her shoulder as she did so. "Yes. I don't know the details because I only arrived yesterday, but I'll be managing the front desk."

And what will I be doing? He was confident Sadie had no clue. In fact, he doubted she knew the answer to any of the dozens of questions running through his mind.

She nodded toward the end of the lobby. "Come on. I'll show you to the conference room where the others are waiting."

Rocco followed behind Sadie, watching the way she bounced slightly with each step and how her ponytail swung back and forth. Her skirt swished with every step. She had energy. The idea that she was a Little floated through his mind again. It was possible, or perhaps just wishful thinking on his part.

Rocco hadn't dated in far too long, and he knew better than to date vanilla women. It was always a mistake. He would never be satisfied in a vanilla relationship in the long run, so why bother entertaining the idea in the short run? All that could happen would be hurt feelings. Probably the woman's when he let her down.

When Sadie reached a door and stopped, he felt a twinge of disappointment. He was about to walk out of her presence. It didn't sit well with him.

"They're in there," she stated.

"Thank you, Sadie," he said softly. "I guess we'll be seeing each other."

She gave him a dimpled smile, and her cheeks turned pink. "Yep."

For reasons he couldn't possibly explain, he reached up and tucked a wayward strand of hair behind her ear. The messy ponytail was already slipping.

Sadie didn't flinch or pull away. Instead, she leaned her cheek into his touch. "Thank you," she murmured before she turned and scampered away like a little bird.

Rocco smiled at her retreating form for several seconds until she disappeared through the door behind the reception desk.

Finally, he took a deep breath to break the spell and reached for the door handle. Whatever the hell was on the other side of this door, it was time to face it.

Chapter Two

Five men looked in his direction as Rocco entered the room. Three were sitting around an oval conference table. Two were standing, leaning against opposite walls. All of them were built and in good shape, like himself. Each man carried himself with the assurance that often came from a military career or advanced defense training. No one spoke.

Rocco looked at each of them in turn as he shut the door behind him. "Who's in charge?"

The group all chuckled.

A dark-skinned man leaning against the wall to Rocco's left spoke first. "We were hoping you were."

Rocco shook his head. "I don't have a clue what I'm even doing here."

"Neither do any of us." The clean-cut-looking man about Rocco's age leaned forward in his chair, held his hand out over the table, and flipped something in the air. He caught it on its way back down and flattened it on the table. "Don't suppose you have one of these?"

Rocco glanced at the gold disc he was well-acquainted

with—a duplicate of the one he'd been carrying in his pocket for two years. He pulled his out now and set it on the table. Each of the other men did, too, including the two men who leaned away from the wall to do so.

"So, we all have a strange gold coin," Rocco stated as if it weren't obvious. "Now what?"

The man closest to Rocco—the one with the broadest chest and bulging muscles—reached for a piece of paper in the center of the table and slid it toward Rocco as Rocco took a seat.

Rocco leaned over the paper. It didn't take him long to read the one line.

Answer the speakerphone on the table at 12:30.

"Informative," Rocco stated sardonically.

The buff man next to him chuckled and held out a hand. "I'm Phoenix."

"Rocco," he said as he shook the man's hand.

"Hawking," chimed in the darker man by the wall.

"Kestrel," added the man who'd flipped the coin onto the table.

"Caesar," grumbled the serious-looking man with a five-day beard similar to Rocco's.

Rocco glanced at the last man, whose face was partially concealed by his baseball cap. After a pause, the man sighed and introduced himself, "Magnus. This is ridiculous."

Rocco had to agree. As he stared at each man, he wondered what had lured them here. Had they each received a letter similar to the one Rocco had gotten last week? More importantly, had their lives been saved at some point, warranting the marker they each possessed?

The phone rang, jerking Rocco out of his wandering thoughts.

Kestrel was closest, so he reached forward and pressed the speaker button. "Hello?"

"Ah, good. Have you all arrived?" came the voice of an older man. He sounded distinguished. Important.

Rocco listened for clues as to where he might be from. There was something formal about his speech. Perhaps he was British.

"How should we know?" Magnus murmured, looking around the room.

"We have," Rocco responded. "At least that's what the reception manager told me."

"Good, good. Let's get right to it then."

"Who are you?" Phoenix asked.

"Who I am is not important. What matters is that each of your lives, or the life of someone close to you, was spared because of my power and contacts."

Rocco looked around the room. Every gaze was the same, glancing at each other. No one refuted the claim.

"You were each given a marker at the time of your rescue. It's time for me to activate you so that you will be in place when the time comes for you to repay it."

Rocco shuddered. "This better not be illegal."

"Oh, my dear man, I can assure you I do not deal in anything that's not for the betterment of society. Let's not get bogged down in legalese. Were you concerned with the law when my men took out those six drug smugglers and disposed of the bodies on the ridge, Mr. Thompson?"

Rocco jumped in his seat. It unnerved him greatly that the disembodied voice in the speaker knew who'd asked the question.

"Now, where were we? Oh, right. Trust me when I say

you were all chosen for a reason. You have skills that will eventually come in handy. You all served in a branch of the U.S. military at one point. You're a team now."

"Skills?" Magnus asked. "I'm a computer geek. I hope you don't expect me to do roof repairs. This building looks like it's falling in on itself."

The voice laughed. "Ah, Mr. Taverson, I assure you the building is not in as much disrepair as it appears. I had an inspector out just last week. It's been vacant for some time, but most of the issues are superficial. A construction team is already working to get the resort up and running as soon as possible."

"So, you intend to reopen this resort? What's our job?" Hawking asked.

"Hawking Winther. Good to hear your voice."

Hawking looked just as unnerved as Rocco felt. Equally unnerved, all of them now glanced around the room, looking for hidden cameras and finding none.

"To answer your question," continued the man, "the resort will reopen in a few weeks. It will be fully operational. Guests will once again stay in the surrounding cabins and the main building. I've assigned the six of you to various jobs around the property, but your work at the resort is mostly a front. Your primary concerns will be unrelated to the resort."

"Pardon?" Caesar grumbled. "You speak in riddles."

"All in due time, Mr. Heskett. All in due time. Your variety of skills will come in handy when the time is right. The reason I chose this location for you all to gather is because it has everything we need to run a separate operation behind the scenes."

"And what the hell is that?" Kestrel asked.

"Mr. Galison... Welcome. You'll need to obtain the building survey from Sadie. You've all met Sadie, I assume?"

Rocco's breath hitched at the reminder. He'd met her all right. It unnerved him that everyone else had, too. At least none of them were smirking or smiling too broadly for his taste. They simply all nodded and murmured their acknowledgment.

"Good, good," the man continued. "She has surveys for you. You'll notice from the original building schematic that entire sections are inaccessible to the public. Most people will not even know some areas exist."

Rocco glanced around as if he could discern any such thing from this conference room. He could not, of course, but he was itching to see what this benefactor of his was talking about.

The man continued. "The entire top floor and the basement of the resort are completely blocked off to anyone whose fingerprints aren't entered in the system or who doesn't have a temporary keycard. You have each been assigned to your own living quarters on the fifth floor. There are six individual apartments and an open communal space, which I believe you will find more than accommodating. The stairs serve as an emergency exit for the guest floors, but the fifth floor and the basement will only be accessible by you.

"Guests will not be aware of your private quarters. Unless, of course, you take someone to your apartment. The building was originally designed to maintain privacy for those working and living inside the resort."

Rocco found himself frowning as he listened. "Please tell me there's a better method of accessing the rooms than the old-fashioned keys I saw out front." Sadie had already told him those were outdated and just for show, but Rocco was feeling surly and a bit argumentative. This entire arrangement was surreal.

The man chuckled. "No, Mr. Thompson, those are

purely decorative. The command center in the basement will be your biggest source of information that will help you protect the resort and its inhabitants."

Rocco's eyebrows lifted. Hell, everyone's did. He was clearly not the only apprehensive person in the room. What kind of protection would guests on vacation need?

"That basement is the primary reason why I purchased this building. It's meant to be used as your home base of operations."

Rocco sat straighter. Operations? Home base? What the hell?

"I've already had the basement outfitted with state-of-the-art equipment, including offices, computers, a kitchen, weight room, and living space. There's even a large-screen television. I want you six to be comfortable and have a place to both work and unwind. It would be prudent if you did not share the existence of the basement with guests. We will decide together if you wish to trust a staff member to clean this area or if you would rather take care of it yourselves to maintain its secrecy."

Rocco was intrigued. Nervous and cautious but intrigued. What did this man have in mind?

"Back to the keys. Sadie has an envelope for each of you. In them are your keycards that access the entry points to the fifth floor and the basement. They also work to get into your rooms. However, you won't need them after today. Mr. Taverson, I trust you can set everyone up so their thumb and finger prints will operate any of the doors on the property."

Magnus flinched. He rubbed his chin, a frown forming on his face. "As long as you have the equipment, I can do that," he agreed hesitantly.

"You will find you have everything you need at the

present. Ask if you discover something I've overlooked or anything new becomes available."

Apparently, Magnus had extensive computer talent. What other hidden talents did these men have?

Rocco cleared his throat. "Why are we in New Zealand. Everyone in this room is American, and your accent is British."

"Ah. You noticed that. If it soothes your curiosity, I have teams such as yours in place all over the globe. There was a hole. I filled it. Now, that's all I'm going to bore you men with for now. Grab your envelopes from Sadie. My expectations are listed inside. Instructions for the immediate future. Please take some time to get acclimated, move into your apartments, and explore the facilities. I'll be in touch."

Silence reigned for long seconds as the call most definitely disconnected.

"What the fuck just happened?" Hawking asked.

Chapter Three

Sadie lifted her gaze toward the conference room. She had no idea what the six men had been meeting about, but she had just given five of them their envelopes as she'd been instructed. One envelope was left. One man had not emerged from the meeting.

She knew his name was Rocco. He'd been the last to arrive. He'd also made her heart stop, and that was not a good thing. She was here for a clean start. She needed this job badly. It had come as a surprise when she'd even been hired, considering the complete lack of references she'd been able to provide.

There had been no way she could have shared anything about her previous job because she hadn't been inclined to take the risk that her new boss would call her former place of employment to inquire about her. Instead of telling the truth, she'd told the man she'd interviewed with that she'd been sexually harassed and just wanted to put it all behind her.

Apparently, he'd bought her story, but she still had no clue why he'd hired her.

When Rocco still didn't appear, she headed in the direction of the conference room. The other men had already collected their envelopes and headed to the top floor where their apartments were located.

Sadie had not been to the top floor. She hadn't been invited to investigate, and snooping around this old building hadn't felt right. Her room was located on the fourth floor. It was like a studio apartment, and she was grateful to have it.

When the new owner had included room and board and benefits with her salary, she'd felt like she'd struck gold. Traveling back and forth into town each day hadn't appealed to her. In addition, she'd had no idea what kind of accommodations she might have found in town.

Sadie took a deep breath as she stepped into the conference room. Something about Rocco made her fidgety. He had an aura about him, a presence. She couldn't put her finger on it, but he was magnetic. And she wasn't at all sure she should let herself get lured in.

She had no idea what the job description was for these six men or what role they played in the reopening of the resort, but she suspected they were a team with a variety of talents who had been hired to manage the property.

Rocco was sitting in one of the comfortable swivel chairs in this extremely out-of-place modern meeting room. He was leaning back casually, staring right at her as if he'd been waiting for her. Had he?

She tucked a wayward lock of hair behind her ear and cleared her throat. "I, uh, brought you your envelope." She held it with a shaky hand. "Is everything okay?" She pointed over her shoulder. "The others went upstairs."

He slowly leaned forward and pushed out the chair next to him. "Come."

The soft command made her mouth dry. That one word

was enough to make her tremble. His tone. The demand. Only one other man had ever spoken to her with such authority, and he'd turned out to be a real jerk.

Sadie shook thoughts of her ex, Lance, from her head. She hadn't thought of him in ages. She'd broken things off with him ten years ago. He had no business occupying space in her head.

Rocco might have issued a similar order, but nothing about him reminded her of Lance. He wasn't angry or even frustrated. He waited patiently for her to obey, his hand on the back of the chair he'd indicated.

Sadie shuffled forward. When she reached him, he carefully held her arm to help her onto the chair. These chairs looked nice, but they were made for grown men. At five-five, only her toes touched the floor.

She handed him the envelope. "I'm supposed to give this to you," she whispered.

Rocco held her with an intense stare, ignoring the envelope entirely as he set it on the table. "How long have you been here at the resort?"

His question caught her off guard. "Uhh, I arrived yesterday."

"Where are you living?"

She swallowed. "I have a room on the fourth floor."

"A room..."

"Like a studio apartment," she amended.

"I see. And you're the reception manager?"

She shifted her weight, feeling the heat of his stare boring into her. "Yes. I mean, I'm in charge of reception. I'll hire other people. It won't be just me."

"I see. Who hired *you*?"

"Uhhh, the owner?"

"You don't know?" His brows drew together slightly.

"Uhhh, I guess not. No." She reached to tuck that dumb lock of hair behind her ear, but it immediately fell back across her cheek. Her hands were shaking, which embarrassed her. She'd managed to be chipper and friendly as the men had arrived earlier. None of the first five had rattled her.

But this man—the last to arrive—had made her heart race. He shouldn't. She needed to ignore the way her body reacted to him. After all, they would be working together. There was no way she would jeopardize her job by drooling over one of her co-workers.

Maybe he was actually one of her bosses. She really didn't know. Sadie needed this job. She also needed to guard her heart against all men. She needed to learn to stand on her own. Falling into old habits by letting someone take care of her was out of the question.

"Do you know his name?"

"The new owner?" Shoot. She'd lost track of the conversation with her wandering thoughts.

He leaned closer. "Yes, Little one, the new owner."

Sadie's breath hitched. Had he just called her *Little one*? She swallowed hard as she held his gaze. Her trembling hand reached to tuck that stubborn lock of hair back again and failed.

Rocco pushed his chair back a few inches. "Come here." He reached for her hand.

She had no idea what his intentions were, but she could no more deny him than her next breath as she set her smaller hand in his and let him help her down from the chair.

"Turn around, Sadie," he encouraged, his voice gentle.

She nearly tripped over her sandals as she spun to face away from him. Why was she obeying him like this? It felt like he'd dug into her deepest special place when he'd demanded she come to him, but he'd flayed her open when he'd called her Little one. Now, she was putty.

"Can you kneel, Little one?"

She twisted her head around to look at him. He was so tall that with him sitting they were nearly eye-to-eye. "Sir?" She shivered as she used the term. It slid out naturally.

He reached for the band in her hair and eased it off, letting the long straight locks tumble down her back and around her shoulders. "Your hair, Little one. It's annoying you. I'm pretty good with hair. Let me fix it."

Her heart raced as she continued to stare at him.

He smiled. A heart-stopping smile that made her want to do anything to ensure he looked at her like that. "I'll be able to reach better if you lower to your knees." He winked at her.

"Oh." As she turned to face away from him again, she lowered onto shaky knees.

He spread his legs and scooted closer as his hands threaded in her hair to finger comb it.

Sadie closed her eyes and pursed her lips, trying not to moan as he divided her hair into three sections and efficiently braided it down her back. When he was finished, he tied it off with the band. "There."

He set his hands on her shoulders and slid them to her biceps. Both her shoulders and her arms were bare because the sundress only had spaghetti straps. Rocco helped her back to her feet and turned her around.

She stood too close to him. She was between his legs. His hands rested on her biceps. Every breath filled her lungs with his scent. Outdoors. Pine. Fresh air. She suspected he always smelled like that, even after a shower. It was heady, and she had to force herself not to step even closer.

"Better?" he asked.

She frowned. What was he referring to?

He reached for her braid and gave it a slight tug.

"Oh, uh, yes. Thank you, Sir." She swallowed and cocked her head to one side. "Do I work for you?"

"I don't think so. I don't know who I work for, Sadie. I was hoping you would tell me."

She chewed on her bottom lip, feeling silly. "I guess I don't know either." She'd taken this job without questioning much.

"I guess we're even then."

"I guess so."

Rocco reached for the chair behind her and pulled it closer so it hit the back of her legs. A second later, he lifted her by the hips and settled her in it himself without a word.

He leaned one elbow on the table next to him and casually bent his head to one side to rest it on his palm. His intense gaze never wavered. "How long have you known you were Little, Sadie?"

His question was so blunt it took her by surprise. Her mouth fell open, but no sound came out. No one had ever confronted her so directly. In fact, she'd never had a conversation about her Little side with a soul outside of the club she'd belonged to years ago in what seemed like another life.

He set his free hand on top of hers, making her realize she had fisted them together in her lap and was twisting her fingers around. "Take a deep breath, Little one. You're safe with me. I promise."

She'd heard that before.

Absolutely nothing about Rocco was reminiscent of Lance though. They shared not a single similarity.

"Answer me, sweetheart." He had the most amazing way of issuing a command in a tone that softened the order.

"I don't know. Since I was a teenager."

"Have you had a Daddy before?"

She bit into her lip and slowly nodded. He was dragging emotions out of her. Emotions she'd rather not share.

Rocco released her hands and sat up straighter to cup her face. His touch was welcome. She craved it like a woman dying of thirst. Like someone who had spent years stuffing her true self deep down and ignoring it.

Rocco Thompson had stripped all her defenses away in seconds and burrowed his way inside. He had the power to destroy her.

"How long ago?" he asked without waiting for an answer.

"Ten years."

His eyes widened. "You haven't had a caregiver in ten years?"

"No, Sir," she whispered. Why did that embarrass her? It shouldn't.

"What happened to that relationship, Little one?"

She shuddered and looked away.

"Sadie..."

"He wasn't a good man. I left."

"Okay. We can talk about that more, later."

She found herself tipping her cheek into his palm.

Oh my God. What are you doing, Sadie?

Shaking some sense into herself, she jumped to her feet and pushed the chair back, nearly stumbling and falling on her butt.

Rocco leaned forward and steadied her with a hand on her wrist.

"I'm sorry," she stammered. "I should get back to work."

He didn't release her wrist though. "Okay, Little one, but look at me first."

She drew in a breath and faced him.

"Don't panic. I won't tell a soul. I can sense something bad happened to you in the past. I'm sorry. I hate when bad

Daddies take advantage of Little girls. It's unconscionable. I know you don't know me, but I promise you I'm not like that man."

"I can't..." She swallowed and forced herself to continue. "I need this job. I can't, uh..."

He nodded. "Okay, Little one. Don't panic. I won't do anything to upset your job. I'm a patient man. I may not have a single clue what this resort is all about or why I'm here, and I suspect you don't either, but I need you to know one thing, Sadie."

She held her breath. She didn't blink as she continued to stare at him as if there was no way to stop it or stop his next words.

"You're mine, Little one."

Chapter Four

Rocco couldn't believe what was happening here. This had not been his intention when he'd remained in this room and waited for her. He'd definitely waited for her, knowing she would seek him out while the others went upstairs.

If he were honest with himself, he'd probably known she was his almost from the moment she'd emerged from the back room. He hadn't been certain if she was Little at that time, though.

The moment she'd stepped into this conference room, her entire presence had called to him. When he'd issued the command for her to come, he'd watched every nuance of her reactions.

That's when he'd known. Known she was Little. Known she was his.

It had unraveled so fast that he had whiplash now. In the span of fifteen minutes, he'd held her between his legs, braided her gorgeous hair, gripped her hands in her lap, stroked her cheek...

If she hadn't spooked and leaped away from him, he

might have kissed her—which probably wouldn't have been his best plan.

She remained in front of him now, letting him hold her wrist. Her green eyes were wide. Her lips parted. She breathed heavily. "Sir, I..."

He slid his hand to hers and clasped her small fingers. "It's okay. I know I just dumped a mountain on you." He needed to reassure her. He smiled, hoping she was feeling his warmth. "We'll take our time, Little one. Get to know each other."

"But..."

He smiled broader. "There really are no buts, sweetheart. You feel it, too." He set his other hand on her chest, his fingers on her neck. "In here. It's a presence. It just happened. I know you need to think and process, and I'm sure you'll have a million questions. I'll answer all of them. Just don't fight it. Can you do that for me, Little one?"

She swallowed.

God, he wished he could push the fast-forward button and get them through this awkward phase, skip over the time she was going to spend freaking out and doubting them both. But this was life. He needed to slow down and guide her gently.

"I need to join the others and make sense of this assignment. I'm sure you need some space and time. I'll come to your room tonight and tuck you in. How does that sound?"

She bit into her lower lip hard enough that he reached up to pluck it from between her teeth before she hurt herself. "That's all I'm going to do tonight, Little one. Tuck you in. If you'd like, I can read you a story."

Finally, she smiled. It wasn't filled with as much sunshine as he knew she was capable of, but it was a start. "Okay," she whispered.

Rocco

Her smile was his undoing, though. That and the fact that she hadn't moved to walk away yet. When she swayed closer and licked her lips, he cupped her face and kissed her. He didn't linger, but the kiss was sweet and soft, and it solidified everything he'd known.

She was definitely his perfect Little girl.

Chapter Five

Sadie turned and walked quickly from the room. She could feel his gaze following her as she tried to exit with her dignity intact. Dignity? What was she thinking? Kneeling at his feet and calling him Sir? She was a royal idiot.

Needing to be away from the desk, Sadie picked up her clipboard of preopening activities. After setting a small sign on the reception desk that gave a number that people could call for assistance, she hurried away to check on one of the myriad of things she needed to take care of today.

Yesterday, she'd worked alone with a few workmen wandering around as they completed tasks on their lists. It had been okay but a little spooky to be alone in this big estate. When the large men started arriving this morning, she'd welcomed them to the estate and personally had felt relief that she wouldn't be the only one there if something went wrong.

I know who I'd go to if I needed help.

"Stop it!" she ordered herself aloud. *Get your mind away from Rocco Thompson.*

Rocco

The first thing on her list was an inventory of the bed linens and consumable materials for the rooms and cabins. Heading for the supply cabinet, she saw one of the men she'd just met. Cursing her poor memory, she flipped to the notes she'd taken after each man had arrived so she could learn their names.

Magnus. Sadie hadn't ever seen his face fully. Thank goodness he always wore a baseball cap, and no one else did, so she could tell at a glance who he was. Armed with his name so she could greet him personally, she turned the corner and found the hallway empty.

She figured he had already taken the elevator, and she'd just missed him. Magnus was obviously a quiet man of few words. Pushing the button to call the elevator, the doors opened immediately, and she stepped in.

As the elevator doors opened on the next floor, Sadie looked down at her list and headed for the supply room. She opened the supply room door and stepped inside to find everything perfectly organized. Thanking whoever had stocked the supplies in such an orderly fashion, Sadie started with the sheets. Each set of sheets, duvet cover, and pillowcases were secured in a cloth bag and stacked on the shelf. She spot-checked five random sets and found them all to be consistent. Housekeeping would only have to stop and pick up the sets for the different size beds. This would take the laundry personnel more time but would be so convenient for the staff working in the rooms.

She quickly completed her inventory. Everything was well stocked except for the bodywash. Whoever had ordered it had obviously thought that one small vial of soap would be sufficient for a room. Guests in a resort like this might shower a couple of times a day after swimming or doing any of the activities that would be available. She made a note to triple

29

the supplies and to have the staff place two bottles of body-wash in each room when they prepped. Otherwise, someone would be making soap deliveries all over the resort.

Taking a few minutes, she set up one cart to illustrate how each of the housekeepers should stock their cart before each shift. Sadie paused to take a picture of the cart. It was possible that the staff would suggest tweaks to her design, and she'd be willing to update the model. She knew they would be the experts, but she was simply providing them with a starting point. Training the staff would be coming soon.

After a quick look around, Sadie smiled. She'd worked in hotel reception years ago, but it had been a while. She was excited to get back to this kind of work, but she knew she would double-check herself for a while to ensure she didn't forget anything.

As she left the supply room, Sadie referred to her list. Her phone buzzed in her pocket, and she froze. She pulled her phone out to look at the caller ID. An unknown number.

"Hello?" she said hesitantly.

"I don't know what the fuck you think you're doing, but I can promise you that trying to..."

Sadie disconnected from the call and stared at the device. How did he keep contacting her? She quickly blocked that number. He must have bought a dozen disposable phones. Briefly debating if she could ignore unknown numbers when they flashed on her screen, Sadie knew she'd have no choice. This was a new job. What if one of the employees or her boss called?

Maybe she could ask for a work phone. Quickly, she added an item to her list to compose an email to her boss. She could word it so he wouldn't know she had a problem.

Relieved, she checked her next item and headed back down to the reception desk to make sure the reservation system was working correctly. Stepping into the elevator, Sadie wondered how busy the resort would be when it opened. Already, she'd seen the slick advertising campaigns the owner was launching in the lucrative U.S. market. Coming to New Zealand was a bucket list item for many people.

If they get to hang out with the hunks I met this morning, everyone is going to want to be here.

Sheer masculinity had radiated from each of the men who had arrived today. She'd tried to keep herself together as she'd spoken to each of them. Even that guy with the computer bags and the baseball cap hiding half his face was evidently in better shape than most athletes. And that last one...

Sadie filed away the image of Rocco that popped into her mind. *Focus!* Pulling herself together as she walked back to the desk, she noted a small package had been left on the counter and knew she'd missed the delivery man. It was addressed to Rocco Thompson. Shaking her head, she decided getting another infusion of Daddy Rocco right now wasn't prudent.

With a crinkle of the packaging, she set it aside to deliver later. Sadie pulled up the reservations system and created a sample reservation. To her delight, she discovered that not only could she successfully book a room, she could schedule classes with the resort experts for lots of experiences. Anything from hikes into the mountain with a picnic to different skill levels of mountain climbing had Rocco's name next to them as the activity coach.

The other men all had activities associated with their names, too. Sadie got lost in the choices as she read all the options. This resort really was a paradise for overworked people who wanted a total escape with a variety of activities.

From stretching out on a chaise lounge under the trees to scuba diving, if people couldn't find something fun to do here, they wouldn't find it anywhere.

She quickly checked off a few activities that sounded fun to try and finished creating the reservation so she could check that the system worked. With a ding, it arrived in the hotel's email system and then went straight through the computer system to register the activity, noting any special requests. Her gaze landed on one section where a message flashed.

ACTIVITY ENROLLMENT FORWARDED AUTOMATICALLY TO THE GUIDE.

The system sends them an email?

She looked to see who was involved with each of the activities. Rocco, Rocco, Rocco... All the activities she had enrolled in, just for practice, were with him! Something inside her panicked, and she furiously pressed buttons on the screen to delete the practice reservation. When a checkmark appeared confirming its removal, Sadie exhaled the breath she hadn't known she'd been holding.

"Hey, Sadie." A deep voice that did funny things to her insides captured her attention, and she looked up from the computer screen to see Rocco walking forward, looking at his phone.

"I just got a list of group activities for mountain climbing experiences."

"Sorry, Rocco," she said quickly. "I sent out a trial reservation. I didn't know it would send a message to you that people were in your classes."

"Mr. Moneybags, his wife Fifi, and their five kids, Sally, Chip, Jeff, Ann, and Peter, were scattered through a bunch." He stopped and looked up at her, his lips twitching. "You're sure these are fake reservations? I'd like to meet someone named Mr. Moneybags."

She scrunched her nose. "Not very original, is it? I've just deleted it. I needed to check that the reservation system was working. The advertisements go live this afternoon."

"It's hilarious. I really wanted to see what Peter Money-bags looked like."

As Sadie searched for something to say, her gaze landed on the package she'd set aside. "This came for you." She quickly handed over the small mailer envelope.

"Wow. I wonder who knows I'm here."

Sadie watched his face change from teasing to serious as he examined the package.

"Who knows? Maybe, it's a welcome gift? Thank you, Sadie," he said, breaking his focus on the item in his hand to look at her.

"You're welcome." She held her breath, waiting for him to excuse himself. To her relief, his focus returned to the package.

He opened it and looked inside before meeting her gaze. "Hey. I'll see you tonight," he said, excusing himself.

"Okay." Sadie focused on the clipboard in her hands and held her breath as he walked away. When he disappeared from sight, air gushed from her lungs. *Damn.* She would have to figure out how to be around him without reacting so strongly to his presence.

Chapter Six

Rocco pulled the flash drive out of the packaging and scrambled to catch the piece of paper that tumbled toward the floor. Looking over the flash drive, he discovered the only clue to its contents was the same symbol on the coin he had been given. Unfolding the paper, he read:

> *Rocco Thompson, your marker has been called into effect. Here is your assignment. Protect Sadie Miller. The encrypted drive contains all the background information I can provide you.*
> *Baldwin Kingsley III*

Rocco's first thought was *Baldwin Kingsley III*... Was that the name of their mysterious benefactor, the man behind all this?

Next, Rocco's dominant personality pushed to the forefront of his mind the idea that Sadie was in trouble. *I need to see what's on this jump drive immediately.* However, he didn't have the equipment to open any encrypted files. Clutching the drive, Rocco jogged to the elevators.

As he reached for the pad to hit floor five, he remembered he would need his keycard to access it. "Ugh. Come on..." he mumbled to himself as he pulled the card from his pocket. Sure enough, floor five lit up, and he was able to select it.

When the elevator opened on the fifth floor, dead silence met him. "Hey! Is the computer guy up here?"

No one answered.

Damn. They must be all downstairs.

Dashing back into the elevator, he stared at the numbers for the floors he could access. Five showed up with his keycard. Not the basement. What triggered the lowest floor? He stared at the display, trying to figure out what to do next.

"How do I get to the damn basement?" he growled. Immediately, the elevator descended. Nothing showed on the display. Was it voice-activated?

When the doors opened, Rocco stepped into the command center. "Whoa!" burst from his lips. As he looked around the room, he tested his memory of the guys he'd met previously, recalling each of their names. They were all extremely fit but so different.

"We wondered when you'd get down here," Phoenix remarked. "Thank goodness Magnus read the directions in the envelope. The rest of us didn't know to say the word 'basement' after using our cards."

Rocco tried to laugh as if he'd definitely known the answer. The look in the other men's eyes told him he wasn't fooling them.

"We're looking at the building specs. There's more to this resort than you think," Kestrel informed him.

"My mission just arrived. All the information is here," Rocco shared, "but it's encrypted. And it would seem our new boss's name is Baldwin Kingsley III. Anyone know who that is?"

They all shook their heads.

"Never heard of him," Magnus muttered. "But I'll do a search and see what I can find."

Rocco headed directly for the computer section. Magnus sat in front of a bank of computers. "Sorry, guy. I need to take your spot for a few."

"Not going to happen. The system activates only for me. Everyone else has tried," Magnus informed him.

"You're our computer genius. Change that," Rocco directed.

"Not happening. I could shut down and rebuild the whole system. Unfortunately, there's a kill command I can't bypass. We'll lose all our intel if I attempt to alter or go around anything," Magnus muttered.

Rocco looked around to confirm his words. Everyone nodded.

"It only works for him," Kestrel confirmed.

Rocco held up the flash drive. "Could you take a look at this and see what's on it?"

Without a word, Magnus plucked the drive from Rocco's fingers and plugged it into the computer. Instantly, a flash of letters and numbers flew across the screen. Magnus leaned forward, watching carefully.

"How long will it take?" Rocco asked quietly, not wanting to disturb the man.

"No clue."

Frustrated by the terse answer, Rocco asked, "Give me more than that."

Shaking his head, Magnus added, "The drive uses a higher-level program, but it appears that the system recognizes it."

A picture opened on the screen. Sadie.

"That's interesting," Caesar said as he walked toward the large display.

Rocco looked around to see that everyone had clustered behind him. Annoyed at their intrusion, he gave everyone a back-off warning look.

"Chill, Dude. We're supposed to be a team, right?" Kestrel pointed out.

Forcing his protective instincts to calm down, Rocco weighed his options. Could he tell the men part of the truth, or would he need to lay everything on the table? "Sorry, guys. Sadie's important to me."

"You just met her. You aren't one of those players who's going to sleep with everyone at the resort, are you?" Hawking asked.

"No. I'm a Daddy who just found his Little girl," Rocco confessed.

"Is that why you really came to New Zealand...to find your daughter?" Kestrel asked.

Rocco grimaced, wondering how much he'd have to explain. "I don't have a daughter. I'm not that kind of daddy. I found my Little girl—as in, my submissive."

"No fucking way," Magnus growled and looked up to meet Rocco's gaze fully for the first time. "I've been looking for mine since I figured out how I was wired. And you've determined the reception manager we just met is your Little?"

Rocco nodded. "Yes."

"Congratulations," Kestrel said with a smile.

Kestrel cleared his throat. When everyone looked at him, Kestrel continued, "I'm guessing we're all Daddies. Has anyone else found their Little?"

One by one, everyone except Rocco shook their heads.

"Do you think Baldwin Kingsley III knows we're all Daddies?" Caesar growled.

"I don't think there's anything that man doesn't know." Magnus gestured at the bank of computers lining the wall. "Anyone who has put this together isn't lacking in information. The guy must be loaded."

"We'll figure that out later. Magnus, show us what's on the file," Rocco urged. The fact that they were all Daddies reassured him that any information contained in the file would be kept confidential.

A picture of a rough-looking man in his mid-fifties appeared on the screen, followed by a list of convictions and suspected accomplices.

"Meet Sylvester Pushkin. As you can see, he's involved in a variety of scams and swindles. Sylvester was Sadie's previous employer."

"I don't like that guy," Rocco muttered.

"You shouldn't. He's the reason she's here. Sadie sent herself a large accounting file on her second-to-last day in his employ," Magnus said, displaying a file.

Screenshots of Sadie's handwritten notes, highlighted in the margins, indicated discrepancies and credits coming from sources outside the United States. The vast majority came from unconfirmed sources in Russia. She'd helpfully noted, *Russian mob?* in red highlight.

"Well, that's not subtle at all," Caesar murmured. "So, they know she suspects they're the bad guys."

"And now, they're after her," Rocco said, shaking his head. Instantly, his mind flashed back to the day he'd gained his marker. He'd had skills but would have died without the help of that team who'd come to his aid. He didn't like that someone had Sadie in his crosshairs, and she certainly needed someone to come to her aid. He would be that someone. Based on the looks on the faces of this entire team of men who'd only met today, they would all have her back.

Kestrel pointed to a report at the corner of the large screen. "There have been several attempts to abduct Sadie or to eliminate her. Your Little is either savvier than she looks, or she's the luckiest woman in the world."

Rocco felt sick. "Do you think she knows?"

"She accepted a job in a foreign country working at a resort with no guests," Hawking pointed out. "Sounds like she's getting as far away as possible from something."

A picture popped up on the screen—Sadie working on the computer, her white teeth worrying her lower lip. With a few keystrokes, Magnus changed the view from her to the monitor she was viewing.

Rocco appeared on her screen.

"Is this live?" Rocco asked.

Magnus nodded. "Yes. I have access to security cameras all over this property. It would seem our benefactor spent a good deal of time and money ensuring the security system and this computer station were decked out with state-of-the-art equipment before he brought us all together."

Rocco leaned forward to see what Sadie was doing. It seemed she had pulled up his personnel file. As he read the information with her, Rocco was relieved to see that the data contained very little information and nothing that indicated that Rocco was anything except a guy with mountaineering experience. As he watched, she adroitly plugged in a drive and copied his information.

"Seems like she often helps herself to information," Caesar commented.

"I'd be suspicious of everyone as well," Rocco said. He was proud of her for being proactive. She'd survived long enough to make it to him.

Magnus pointed to a green light at the top of Sadie's picture. "There's no chatter on the web now about her. That light will change when the computer picks up something. I'll start digging into her old boss. Considering his current criminal activity, there's no way this is his first rodeo. I bet that guy has a history of breaking the law. Nailing him down for a long list of crimes might be the best way to put an end to the threat against Sadie."

Rocco nodded. Magnus had a good point. The easiest way to get this asshole off his Little girl's back would be to ensure he got arrested and taken out of commission. All Rocco needed was a bit of patience. He would do everything in his power to protect Sadie, but in the end, they would need to take down Sylvester Pushkin.

"Can you leave that indicator up?" Rocco requested. "And could I have a copy of that information to study?"

"Give me a minute." Magnus typed commands into the computer. "I've sent it to your Danger Bluff email."

"I have a Danger Bluff email?" Rocco asked.

"We were all set up with social media, email, and phones," Caesar shared. "All the information is in your locker. It opens with your fingerprint. We were going to come get you in a while to get your prints in the system, but you were busy."

Rocco looked back at Magnus. "You've got eyes all over the resort? Inside and out?"

"Everywhere but the creepy places." With a few keystrokes, Magnus changed the large display of Sadie at work to a view of the exterior of the building for a few seconds before it rotated to display the interior again. "No bathrooms, bedrooms, etc. Everywhere else shows up on the screens."

"What is Kingsley expecting to happen here?" Rocco asked, looking at each man gathered around him.

"That's a very good question that we've all asked. There must be a threat we need to prepare to handle," Phoenix suggested.

"Possibly more than one," Caesar added.

Rocco nodded. "I'm just going to ask. Is there anything the team needs to know about any of you?"

No one offered any information but looked steadily back at him.

"Then I'm going to trust each of you. It seems like we need to have a team we can rely on. Any suggestions of where we start?"

"You need to explore the contents of your locker. The rest of us are a step ahead of you," Magnus informed him. "Before you do that, let's get your prints in the system so you won't have to guess *Open Sesame* next time in the elevator."

Rocco stepped forward and lifted his hand to the machine.

Within seconds, the computer whiz nodded at him. "You're done."

"Thanks. I'll check out my locker down here. Then I guess I also need to ensure the climbing equipment is in good shape and secure it," Rocco said.

"We were all just heading out," Kestrel said. "I vote we have dinner together each day. Tonight, let's talk about any security risks we see in our areas. We need to stay connected and informed. If nothing happens and we get sick of each other, we can drop the idea."

The others nodded their agreement.

Chapter Seven

A large pot of spaghetti sat in the middle of the table in their common area in the basement. Since Kestrel had suggested having dinner together, he'd ordered and picked up the food from the rudimentary kitchen where the chefs were trying out recipes. They'd set everything on a cart, and Kestrel had escorted it down the elevator. When the doors had opened, the delicious smell alone had lured everyone to their dining area.

Rocco looked at the other five men filling the sturdy chairs at the table. With a shrug, Magnus stood and helped himself to a heaping plate of pasta before passing the dish to Phoenix. The silence in the room made the scraping of serving utensils seem deafening.

Phoenix was the first to break the silence. "Considering what we learned today about Sadie, I think we can safely assume we're going to be dealing with some challenging assignments, which means we probably need a game plan that includes beefed-up security from every angle of this resort."

Rocco couldn't agree more, especially considering the first assignment wasn't just a random woman who happened to be the reception manager. She was his Little. He had no doubts. He'd gone through the motions of familiarizing himself with his assigned task throughout the day, but he'd never gotten her out of his mind, and he couldn't wait to see her again after the team finished their dinner.

Phoenix glanced at Rocco before continuing, "I'll start. I'm in charge of maintenance. I used to be a fireman, so I'm always looking for areas of concern. I found a few safety issues that I'll deal with, but mainly, I was impressed by the setup. There's a maintenance schedule that's online and automated. I also have a monthly printed schedule of everything that needs to be done," he said as he piled his plate full. "I'll rely on you all to tell me if some maintenance issue appears in your area of expertise."

"I'll work closely with you, Phoenix," Hawking said as he accepted the spaghetti fork to help himself next. "I'm a weapons expert, but here, I'm in charge of security. This is a huge area, and there are multiple entry points—by road, sea, and the cliff. It will be pretty much a security nightmare when the resort is full of guests. I can see that having Magnus's eyes on everything will be a great benefit. But he has to sleep sometime."

He paused to look down at the fork in his hand. "What is this? Like the magic talking stick from kindergarten? We can only talk if we have this in our hands?"

The laughter that followed broke some of the tension. Rocco relaxed back against his chair for the first time since the group had met for dinner and noted that the others did as well.

Grinning, Hawking continued, "Magnus, you go next because I see security and IT working closely together. How can I view what you see here when I'm outside or in my quarters?"

"No one will have access to everything I see," Magnus told the group. "But, I can set up a smaller feed of the perimeter to allow your security staff to monitor the area twenty-four/seven."

"That would be better than nothing. I can always come here or contact you if I need to see what's happening," Hawking finished and pushed the lightened pot of spaghetti to the next guy.

Caesar jumped in next as he helped himself. "I'm in charge of water exploration here. My background is in underwater sports. The setup for scuba and snorkeling is secure. All the equipment can be locked up when not in use to avoid tampering. I explored the shoreline from about a half mile out. There are a series of caves that could harbor assailants. I suggest we get waterproof surveillance for those entrances," he said. "Then we can keep an eye on them."

"Added to my list," Magnus said, typing into his phone.

Kestrel followed. "The helicopter is almost brand new. It's better than something that has never flown. It has just enough miles to tell me it's reliable without needing constant maintenance. The bird's-eye view may come in handy—even more so if we add a thermal imaging camera to my display."

Magnus added that to his list. "What else?"

Kestrel added, "I suspect we need to add lighting to the helicopter pad. I'm sure it's limited so the cabins nearby aren't illuminated at night, but I think there will be too many shadows around it if we're worried about sabotage. We'll have to judge how much danger we're expecting."

"That seems to be the million-dollar question. How safe does safe have to be?" Rocco spoke up. "I'm in charge of hiking and climbing. I hiked the trails today, and the upper levels of that cliff face will be survivable by only the most skilled mountain climbers with the best equipment and plenty of time to attach anchors."

"But for descent from the top? Is that doable?" Hawking asked.

"With a long enough rope, definitely. It would take some time for someone to navigate down that cliff face safely. There's likely to be debris dropping from their path. Falling stones and earth will warn us someone is coming," Rocco pointed out.

"So, the easiest way to get into the resort is to drive through the front gates as a guest or delivery person," Kestrel said to sum up their findings.

"There's a big dock out there. I would guess that a good restaurant could draw people in on boats," Caesar said.

Everyone looked at the pasta that was quickly disappearing. Hawking confiscated the pasta fork and filled his plate again. Rocco knew they would definitely have day visitors as well if the chefs could create food as delicious as this dish.

"There's another thing we need to discuss," Magnus said after a short lull in the conversation.

Rocco shifted his full attention to the computer genius.

"Baldwin Kingsley III is in the wind," Magnus informed them.

Rocco flinched. "What does that mean?"

Magnus shrugged. "It means he doesn't exist. Not on paper, at least. Could be a pseudonym. Could be that the guy is just so loaded he keeps his name hidden from the globe. Whatever the case, I have no information to share about him, and I doubt I ever will."

There was a collective sigh.

Kestrel ran a hand over his hair. "Do you think this should worry us?"

Magnus leaned back in his chair and sighed. "Not really. It doesn't change anything. Whoever the guy is, he obviously doesn't like public attention. We all know he sent teams of people to rescue our asses from precarious situations. We owe him a marker. His primary goal seems to be to save the innocent out of the goodness of his heart. If he has any ulterior motives, I don't know what they are."

Rocco nodded. "I don't think we have much choice but to trust him and do our jobs." He felt a bit anxious since the first task was obviously meant for him, and he had a personal interest in the woman he'd been assigned to protect.

It seemed crazy and farfetched, but Rocco had the feeling Kingsley was some omniscient matchmaker—madness, of course. No one could possibly be that all-knowing.

With the official business conducted for the evening, Rocco changed the subject. It was time for everyone to get to know each other. "Hawking, are there enough weights in the workout area for you? You must bench press a small vehicle."

His target laughed and flexed a bicep for them. "Don't be a hater, Rocco. The girls go crazy for my muscles. Probably as much as they do for your good looks."

"I'm only hoping one Little girl is affected by my charm," Rocco tossed back.

"What is Sadie up to tonight?" Kestrel asked.

"Hopefully, she's planning an early evening," Rocco responded.

Sadie let herself out the resort door and into the warm evening air. She'd spent too much time indoors today and needed a break. Wandering through the gardens, she admired all the beautiful plants that lined the path. A flock of gardeners had descended on this green space to whip it back into shape. She definitely could see the improvements they'd made.

Taking a seat on one of the benches, she looked up at the moon and marveled that it didn't look a bit different than it had back in the States. However, the air might be cleaner than in the large cities Sadie always ended up in. She loved working in a place so different from her last job, taking care of the books in that basement office. She'd forgotten how much more entertaining it was to work in reception. The variety. Talking to people. The challenges.

She rolled her eyes at that dismal space she'd been working in most recently. Things had gotten even worse when she'd discovered that the accounts hadn't been balancing. Sadie hadn't understood why Sylvester Pushkin had assigned her to work temporarily in the accounting department after hiring her for a management position. That confusion had grown when lots of time had passed, and he hadn't seemed to be in a hurry to remove her from accounting.

At first, it had been a dream job. The person training her on their system had coached her through the process, feeding her the information and how to enter data into the software. When it had seemed confusing, Sadie had done some online research. With every bit of knowledge she'd gained, their process had seemed increasingly...wrong.

When she'd questioned how to handle the data, Sylvester had called her into his office. Talking to him that time had scared Sadie to the core.

"A bit of knowledge is a dangerous thing, Ms. Miller. We have a system here, and I expect you to follow it, chalking up any questions you have to your lack of experience. I don't pay you to ask questions. Do you understand me?" he had asked, glowering at her from across the scarred wooden desk.

If she hadn't, the sight of the men flanking him behind his desk had done the job. They'd looked like they could rip her head off and not feel any remorse. They probably had already done that to someone... or several someones.

"Yes. I understand, sir. My apologies. I'll get back to work now," she'd said quickly to excuse herself.

Sadie hadn't waited for him to dismiss her. She'd dashed from the room, heart pounding. Returning to her office, Sadie had thrown herself into her work. As the weeks had passed, a replacement hadn't come. She'd had no intention of revisiting Mr. Pushkin's office, so she'd kept working.

As usual, curiosity had been her downfall. Concealing a second set of accounts in a hidden folder on her computer and emailing the results to her personal email, she'd dealt with the official accounts as her online training had taught her. The results had been undeniable. Something had been rotten in the approved method of accounting. She'd taken a big chance in sending the discrepancies between the two sets of books to her personal email, but she'd wanted to protect herself if Sylvester had tried to prove she'd been the one doctoring the books on her own.

That last day she'd come in, Sadie had known something was terribly wrong. As she'd walked through the other cubicles to reach the closet-like office where she'd worked, Sadie had caught the side looks and felt everyone watching after she'd passed. Casually, she'd glanced back over her shoulder when she'd stopped to open her door and found a number of people staring at her. With a wave, she'd disappeared inside.

Her computer had vanished from her desk and a note had instructed her to pick it up from IT. Turning around, she'd headed to that department on the other side of the building. The looks and whispers had followed her once again.

Sadie had darted into a bathroom to give herself a few minutes. Making up an excuse to return to her car, she'd washed her hands and exited the bathroom. At the door, two large men had stepped in front of the exit, trapping her inside.

"I forgot my phone in my car," she'd said quickly.

"You won't need that for work, anyway," one had told her in a heavy tone that cut off any argument.

She'd turned and walked down the hallway to the IT department. Rounding a corner to the right, Sadie had braced herself against the wall. She'd had no doubt that the gurus in the computer section would not have wanted to talk to her, but someone else would.

A door banging had made her jump and automatically look for the source. The janitorial service had arrived and were entering and leaving from the emergency door. Without hesitating, Sadie had tucked herself in between the two men hauling garbage outside. The moment her feet had touched the pavement, she'd taken off at a run.

The call of a bird in the New Zealand night sky startled her from the memories. Sadie pressed a hand against her chest and felt her heart pounding from the fright that day still provoked. Pushing away the horrible nightmare, she stood and walked back to the entrance.

She hadn't seen the guys for hours. *They must be early birds*, she decided, looking up to see the rooms on the top floor were black. Sadie felt better having them around. Last night, she'd been the only one inside the resort's hotel. The creaking floors of the old main house had kept her awake until the wee hours.

Riding in the elevator to her apartment on the fourth

floor, Sadie slumped against the door. She hoped this place would be far enough away that Sylvester wouldn't find her. New Zealand was a beautiful place. She could stay here for a while.

In a short time, she was locked safely in her room. Sadie went straight to her bed. She'd risked going to her apartment that fateful day for only two things. Her home computer and Edgar, her stuffie from childhood. The bedraggled penguin was bald in a few places and floppy. None of that mattered. Edgar was her oldest friend, and he kept the bad things away.

As always, she ran through the highlights of her day with Edgar. "The men came. They talked to whoever owns this place. I couldn't hear what was happening, but they looked totally different when they came out than when they entered —like someone had turned on a lightbulb inside them. He must have told them what their jobs would be here at Danger Bluff."

"Then... Then *he* kissed me and tricked me into telling him I was a Little girl."

When Edgar looked at her funny, she admitted, "Okay, he didn't trick me. He put off these Daddy vibes that are too hard to resist. Somehow, he knew everything about me."

Hugging Edgar closely, she added, "He's a really good kisser. Like a twelve on a scale of one to ten. I think he might be my Daddy. I'm going to be careful because I can't trust anyone."

Chapter Eight

A sudden knock at Sadie's door made her jump to her feet. Her heart was racing as she stared at the door. No one had ever come to her room at night since she'd arrived at the resort.

Finally, she remembered Rocco had said he would come to her apartment tonight. How could she possibly have forgotten that?

She knew the answer. She'd blocked it out of her head as soon as he'd told her so that she wouldn't spend the rest of the day hoping he would really come.

"Sadie?"

At the sound of Rocco's voice, she rushed over to the door and opened it. "Hey."

He smiled at her. He was holding a single rose. "Please tell me you didn't forget I was coming tonight." His voice was teasing, but he lifted a brow.

She swallowed. "I, uh..."

Both his eyes went wide, and his smile faded. "You did forget?"

She shook her head and admitted softly, "No. I just didn't permit myself to believe you would come."

He took a step closer. "May I come in, please, Little girl?"

She hurried to back up, holding the door wider. "Yes. Of course."

He held out the single rose. "There isn't exactly a florist nearby, so I cut this from the garden. Hopefully, no one will notice." He winked.

"It's so pretty. Thank you." She reached for it, but he pulled it back.

"It has a lot of thorns, sweetheart. Why don't you let me stick it in a glass of water for you. Roses are pretty, and you may lean over and inhale the scent, but I don't want you to nick your skin."

Sadie nodded and spun around to head for the kitchenette in her little studio. She suddenly realized she was still holding Edgar and blushed deeply as she tried to set him discretely on the small counter.

After she filled a glass with water, Rocco set the rose in it before nodding toward her stuffie. "Are you going to introduce me to your special friend?"

Her cheeks heated deeper as she stared at Rocco, wondering if he was mocking her. He didn't look like he was making fun, so she set the glass on the counter and picked up the penguin. "This is Edgar. I've had him most of my life."

Rocco lifted a hand to pat the penguin on the head. "Nice to meet you, Edgar. I hope you don't mind sharing Sadie with me." He leaned in closer to whisper directly in Edgar's ear. "She's very special to me. I feel so lucky to have met her today. I promise to treat her like a princess."

Sadie couldn't help but smile as Rocco spoke to her penguin. His words helped calm her racing heart. He really seemed like one of the good guys. But was there such a thing as "good guys"?

Her history would suggest otherwise, but she should probably give Rocco the benefit of the doubt, assuming he really was here to read her a story and not to try to get her into bed.

"Are you just hitting on me because I'm the only woman at the resort so far, and you want to be the first of the men to get me into bed?" she blurted skeptically. She didn't feel apologetic for her question. She needed to be brave, bold, and upfront.

Rocco shook his head. "No, Little girl. I'm not hitting on you at all. The connection between us is already solid. I know you feel it, too. And none of the rest of my team will be making a move on you. I can assure you of that."

She flinched. "Why? Am I not attractive enough?"

His eyes went wide. "Sweetheart, you're the most attractive woman I've ever seen in my life. The rest of the guys know I feel that way. That's why they won't be vying for your attention. I already told them you were mine."

Still feeling defensive because she thought she should, Sadie crossed her arms defiantly, tucking Edgar under one elbow. "That was awfully possessive of you."

"Mmm-hmm." He lifted a hand and slowly cupped her face.

She instinctively tipped her cheek into his palm. His touch calmed her and made her feel silly for questioning him.

"Do you think Edgar will mind if I help you get ready for bed, tuck you in, and read you a story?"

Sadie shook her head. "He likes stories."

"Good." Rocco slid his hand down from her cheek, over her shoulder, and lower until he clasped her hand. "Where are your jammies, sweetheart?"

"In my dresser."

Rocco guided her to the small dresser. "Pick something out, Little one."

When he let go of her hand, she missed his touch immediately. She quickly opened the second drawer and selected a lightweight pajama set. The long-sleeved top and pants were soft cotton and covered with penguins.

"I'm sensing a pattern here," Rocco commented, a bit of laughter in his voice.

"I like penguins," she admitted.

"They are very cute animals. Did you know the daddy emperor penguin tucks the egg under him and balances it on his feet for months, guarding it with his life?"

Sadie nodded, wide-eyed, surprised Rocco knew so much about penguins. "I've seen that in documentaries. It's so sweet."

Rocco reached up a hand to cup her face. "Daddies can be fierce protectors."

She knew her eyes remained wide while she held his gaze.

"I want you to know that you can count on me to defend you at any cost, too."

For several heartbeats, they stared at each other before Sadie whispered, "We just met." She suddenly felt guilty for entertaining the idea that she could enter into any kind of relationship with Rocco. Besides the fact that he was a coworker, she'd come all the way to New Zealand to hide. What would Rocco think if he found out she was on the run? She would never expect anyone to understand. There was no way she would tell him about her predicament. She was hoping it would go away, actually. Surely her previous employer would eventually grow tired of looking for her and stop calling.

Rocco

"I know you feel the connection, Sadie," Rocco said. He set a hand on her chest. "In here."

She nodded slowly, unable to deny the truth of his words or her agreement.

You should tell him to go. You can't date a man you work with, or any other man for that matter.

She glanced at the door.

"Sadie, look at Daddy."

She jerked her gaze back to his, her breath catching when he called himself Daddy.

His brow was slightly furrowed. "Do you want me to leave?"

She hesitated and slowly shook her head. She never ever wanted him to leave. But was this wise? Should she tell him about her problems?

No. She'd just started this job. The last thing she wanted to do would be to risk her employment. What if Rocco told her boss, and he decided she was a liability? She could end up fired and on the street in a foreign country without enough funds to even leave the island.

"I don't think it's a good idea to date coworkers," she finally managed to blurt out. Her chest hurt with the admission. She so badly didn't want this kind man to leave.

"We aren't dating, Sadie. Not in the traditional sense." He stepped closer and pulled her into his arms.

She held her jammies and Edgar against her chest.

"I know it happened fast between us, but this is already a relationship. I'll speak to Mr. Kingsley to make sure he's aware."

She frowned. "Who is Mr. Kingsley?"

He smiled. "Apparently, he's our boss. I found out his name earlier today. Baldwin Kingsley III, to be exact."

55

"Oh. Do you think it's weird that I took this job without knowing his name?" she asked.

Rocco chuckled. "We all did, sweetheart."

"Oh, right." She giggled.

"Anyway," Rocco continued. "I'll speak to Kingsley about our relationship."

She gasped as she realized what he intended to do. "Oh no. Don't do that. We might get fired."

"We won't get fired, Little one. I promise."

She tried to step back, but she was caught in Rocco's strong embrace.

"Sadie," he continued, "no one is getting fired. I promise."

She shook her head, feeling more nervous by the moment. Reality seeped in. She was all alone in this world. She needed this job. She needed to be in New Zealand, where Sylvester Pushkin couldn't find her.

"Take a breath, sweetheart," Rocco ordered. "You're safe."

She pursed her lips. His choice of words was too close to home. She wasn't safe. She might never be safe again.

"You need to get to bed, Little girl. Do you want Daddy to change your clothes for you, or would you like to go in the bathroom and get ready on your own tonight?" Rocco released his hold on her.

She was tired. Not just because it was the end of a long day but also because she hadn't slept well in weeks. She couldn't think of anything more enticing than having an amazing Daddy put her to bed, but getting naked in front of him was out of the question. *Shake out of it, Sadie.*

"I can do it," she murmured.

"Good girl." He gently turned her around so she was facing the small bathroom. "I'll pick out a story."

She glanced at the empty bookshelf along one wall. "I

haven't had a chance to get any new books since I arrived in New Zealand." She winced at the thought of all her favorite books that had been abandoned in her apartment. Some of them had been dog-eared and special to her.

"I guess we'll need to rectify that soon. But for tonight, I'll find something I already have downloaded on my phone. How does that sound?"

She smiled. He looked so sincere. "Okay."

Rocco turned her around and gave her a pat on the bottom.

Sadie rushed into the small bathroom and shut the door. Leaning against it, she stared at herself in the mirror.

There was a battle of wills going on in her head. She knew it was a horrible idea to get involved with someone. She knew she was basically lying to him by omission. But she was also so drawn to him.

She'd never felt this kind of pull to a Daddy. Or anyone, for that matter. It felt so good. She couldn't deny him. Not tonight, anyway. What harm could it do to let someone else take care of her for one evening?

After quickly changing into her jammies, she brushed her teeth and washed her face. Rocco was about to see her without makeup. She didn't wear much—just some mascara and lip gloss—but as the reception manager, she needed to look somewhat professional. Though her lashes were dark, they were also sparse and looked very different with her thickening mascara.

Stop stalling. Sadie took a deep breath and turned to face the man who'd insisted he was her Daddy.

Chapter Nine

Rocco waited patiently while Sadie was in the bathroom. He knew she was probably standing in there, going over the pros and cons of the wisdom of letting him into her life.

What Sadie didn't fully understand yet was that she was indeed his already. She could fight it and toss every excuse in the book at him, but in the end, she would be his Little girl.

He suspected part of her inner turmoil stemmed not from her arguments that the two of them had just met or even from her concern about dating a coworker. Sadie was hiding something from him, and it undoubtedly wore on her.

She wasn't ready to hear that he already knew her secrets and probably knew more about her recent past than she did. He wouldn't bring it up tonight. She needed sleep.

It was true that he needed to speak to Mr. Kingsley about his relationship with Sadie and make sure his odd, mysterious benefactor understood that she wasn't just an assignment. He wouldn't be asking for permission or approval. Rocco would be putting his foot down on this issue. Kingsley would have to get over himself if he had a problem with Rocco's plan.

Rocco

When the bathroom door opened and Sadie stepped cautiously into the main room, Rocco stood from her bed and held out a hand. "Come, Little one."

She shuffled closer.

When she reached him, he slid a palm up her arm. She looked slightly different, and he realized she'd been wearing mascara earlier. She looked just as pretty without it. Fresh and sweet.

"Are you going to kiss me?" she blurted adorably.

"Would you like me to kiss you?" Rocco asked, smiling. He was so totally going to kiss her before tucking her in, but he liked the idea of her asking for it.

She chewed on the corner of her bottom lip and nodded.

Rocco lifted his hand to her face and pulled her lip free of her teeth before closing the distance and kissing her while both hands snaked around her.

He took his time, keeping it tender at first while he nibbled around her lips and found out how good she felt in his arms.

It was cute how she held Edgar against her chest with one arm while she leaned into him and rose onto her tiptoes. When she let out a small whimper, he licked the seam of her lips and took the kiss deeper.

He wouldn't do more than kiss her tonight but wasn't ready to break this connection either. He wanted more. She tasted so sweet, and she was so pliant in his arms. Even though he knew she had a pile of hesitations in her head, she was ignoring them to kiss him. She felt every bit of the connection.

As badly as Rocco wanted to slide his hands around, cup her breasts, and learn more about her body, he stopped himself and broke the kiss, meeting her gaze.

They were both breathing heavily, and that pleased him.

"Let's get you tucked in, Little temptress," he teased as he forced himself to step back and pull the comforter down.

Her cheeks were flushed as she hurried to climb under the covers. "You're really going to read me a story?" she asked, surprise in her voice.

"Of course. Daddies don't go back on their word, Little one."

She giggled as she curled up on her side, tucking Edgar in against her chest.

Rocco sat on the edge of the bed next to her hips. "I found a cute story in my e-reader. It's kind of long, but I bet if I read it to you every night for a few weeks, we'll get through it."

Her eyes widened in astonishment. "You're going to come to my room every night?"

He leaned over and kissed her forehead. No. He wouldn't be coming to her room for more than a few nights. By then, he intended to have her moved into his apartment upstairs. He hadn't taken the time to explore the personal space assigned to him yet, but he did know there were two bedrooms. One of those would get turned into a playroom for Sadie. In fact, he intended to start on that project as soon as he tucked her in.

"Yes. I'll always tuck you in, Little one. I wouldn't be a very good Daddy if I didn't help you get ready for bed and read you a story, would I?"

She blinked. "I don't really know. I've never had a good Daddy before."

"Well, that's one of my jobs. It's in the Daddy rule book."

She giggled again. "That's not a real thing."

He gasped as if astonished. "Of course, it is. It's rule number three, right after keeping Little girls safe and disciplining them if they misbehave."

Rocco

Her eyes went wide, and her jaw dropped open. She also squirmed delightfully under the covers and hugged Edgar closer as she rolled to her back. "You're planning to discipline me?"

"Yes. When you need me to, Little one." He let that hang between them, enjoying how she squirmed further, her pretty mouth opening and closing.

"Why would I need you to discipline me?" she finally asked. Her curiosity was painted on her face. She'd never been in a healthy age-play relationship before. She'd told him as much earlier.

He reached for her free hand and brought it to his lips to kiss her knuckles. "All Little girls are different, Sadie. I can't know yet how often you'll want me to discipline you, what form you'll prefer, or how you might decide to misbehave to get what you crave."

Her eyes had been wide before. Now, they bugged out. She also squeezed her legs together under the covers. "Do you mean like...spanking?"

"Yes, if that's what you enjoy."

She scrunched up her face. "Why would I want you to spank me?"

He chuckled. He was enjoying her reactions so much that he decided to push further. "Most Little girls like the release of endorphins they get from having their bottoms swatted until they're pink and hot. It's cathartic. It's not for everyone, though. Some Littles don't like pain, or they've had a bad experience with spanking or impact play in their pasts. They might respond better to timeouts or writing sentences or even orgasm denial."

Her entire body flinched as she shoved back and sat upright, dropping Edgar to her lap.

Rocco set his palm on one of her thighs, giving no reaction to her sudden shocked movements. While she was off balance, he asked, "Have you ever been spanked, sweetheart?"

She shook her head. "No, Sir."

Oh, how he loved the way she said *Sir*. She was submitting to him beautifully right now. He wasn't sure she was aware of all the telltale signs her body language was putting off. She was so turned on she was shaking.

"You've thought about it, though," he pointed out, lifting a brow.

Her mouth opened and closed again several times before she licked her lips. Finally, she drew in a breath. "Yeah, but those are just thoughts."

"That's understandable. Unless you've spanked yourself in the past, you haven't had anyone to do so yet. Now you do, and we'll explore that path together, Little one. I promise Daddy will watch you closely the first time I spank you to ensure you're reacting appropriately." He gave her thigh a squeeze.

"What, uh... What is the appropriate way for an adult to react when they're spanked?"

"Depends on if it's a naughty girl spanking you need to help purge stress and tension or if it's a maintenance spanking for the purpose of pleasure." Rocco had had no intention of having this conversation with Sadie tonight, but it had happened anyway, and he needed to roll with the punches and answer her questions to soothe her curiosity. If not, she would lie awake panicking after he left.

She blinked several times. "I don't know what that means."

He released her thigh and set his hand on the other side of her legs so they were face to face. "I'll give you an example. Let's say you have a stressful day at work. Everything goes wrong. Two people call in sick. The linens turn pink in the washer because someone dropped a red tablecloth in with the white sheets. A water heater breaks, and ten people come to the front desk complaining. You'd feel pretty stressed at the end of that day, wouldn't you?"

She nodded and cocked her head to one side. "What does that have to do with a spanking?"

"At the end of such a day, when Little girls come home to their safe space, it's not unusual for them to misbehave intentionally. Throwing toys or having a tantrum or refusing to eat dinner."

She frowned.

He smiled. "They do those things in order to earn a spanking. The spanking helps chase away the stress from a long day of problems."

She stared at him for several seconds. "I guess that makes sense, sort of. I can't imagine ever doing something like that."

"You've never had a safe place where you *could* do something like that. You've never had a loving Daddy you knew you could trust to take care of you."

"I guess."

"Then there's the other kind of spanking. A maintenance spanking."

"What does that mean?" She was so inquisitive. He loved her innocence.

"It means you can skip the naughty behavior and simply come to Daddy and ask for a spanking because you crave the release you know you'll get. Chances are, either type of spanking will make your pussy wet and needy. The difference is that when you misbehave to earn the spanking, you're far less likely to get the other kind of release you crave. An orgasm. Whereas, if you ask for a maintenance spanking, Daddy will be happy to thrust his fingers into your sweet pussy and let you come afterward." He leaned forward and kissed her nose.

Sadie gasped. After another second, she lowered onto her back again and pulled Edgar to her chest as if he might comfort her. She rubbed his small beak with her fingers. It looked like it had probably been a smooth, shiny material years ago. It had worn down from years of comforting its owner, though.

"I don't know about all that," she murmured.

"I wouldn't expect you to, sweetheart. Like I said, we'll explore together when you're ready. How about if I read the first chapter of our story now? I think you're going to enjoy it."

"What's it about?" she asked, settling into the bed more comfortably with the change of subject.

"It's about a Little girl who wants to go to the zoo to see the penguins, but the zoo in her town doesn't have penguins, so she takes a long trip to get to a bigger zoo with more animals."

Sadie slowly smiled and then giggled. "You're teasing me."

Rocco held up his phone. "Nope. I wouldn't joke about a good book."

"Why do you have a book for Little girls on your phone?" she asked.

"I have lots of books for Little girls on my phone. A Daddy must always be prepared to tell a story when his Little girl needs one."

"Is that in the rule book for Daddies?" she asked, giggling again.

"Of course. It's in the top ten." He leaned over to give her one more kiss on the lips before opening his phone to start the story.

She listened intently with a beautiful smile on her face until he got to the very end of the first chapter. Her eyes grew heavy-lidded, and she was struggling to stay awake, so Rocco ended there, reminding himself he would have to back up a few paragraphs tomorrow night.

He rose to his feet, kissed her forehead, and whispered, "Sweet dreams, Little one. See you tomorrow."

After turning out the lights, he exited her room, letting the door shut slowly so it wouldn't slam and disturb her.

He was grinning as he headed down the hallway toward the stairwell leading to the private, secured floor where his apartment was located.

When he stepped out into the common area, he found the rest of the guys lounging on the giant sectional and surrounding armchairs. They all looked up as he entered.

"Did you lecture her about wandering around in the gardens alone?" Magnus asked before Rocco had a chance to say a word.

Rocco sighed. "No. I will tomorrow. We had other things to discuss, and I didn't want to explain how I knew she was in the gardens tonight."

Magnus grunted.

"You have a point," Hawking said. "She might not be too thrilled when she finds out Magnus can surveil her at all hours of the day and night."

Rocco flinched and narrowed his gaze, looking toward Magnus. "There aren't any cameras inside her apartment, are there?"

Magnus shook his head. "No. But I'll know if she leaves her room. There are cameras in the hallways."

Rocco nodded toward the hall leading off this common area where their individual apartments were located. "What about our private quarters up here? Any cameras in there?"

"No cameras on this floor except outside the door in case someone approaches who isn't supposed to be up here."

Kestrel shuddered visibly. "Glad to hear that. I'd be a bit squicked out if I thought I was being filmed everywhere."

Rocco had an agenda to discuss before dropping into bed. "I noticed my apartment has two bedrooms. Do all of them?"

"Yes," Phoenix responded. "At least, mine does."

Everyone else nodded.

Rocco wasn't sure how they were going to respond to his next statement, but it couldn't be avoided. Since they had established all six of them were Daddy Doms, surely they wouldn't judge him.

He rubbed the back of his neck as he continued, "I'm going to turn that second room into a playroom for Sadie. I hope it won't be too difficult to get furnishings and other supplies delivered."

Caesar sat forward. "I doubt it would be a problem. However, it won't be necessary to order furniture. It would seem our mysterious benefactor is well aware of our proclivities. I found an invoice in a folder on the kitchen table itemizing a long list of supplies due to arrive tomorrow. It included six twin beds, dressers, bookshelves, and a few other items."

Rocco was stunned. "He already ordered furniture for future Littles?" That seemed presumptuous.

"It would seem so," Hawking added. "Looks like we'll be doing some assembling in the next few days. We'll start with your playroom and work our way around to the others. No rush on those since there aren't even any women around this resort yet, and even if there were, there'd be no guarantee they'd be Little."

Kestrel nodded. "I have a suspicion we will all eventually be meeting the perfect Little girl."

Rocco

Rocco glanced around this common room, wondering how long the six of them might be living here. "Does anyone else find it interesting that Kingsley is going to great lengths to make us feel at home, considering we are technically off the hook once we repay the marker we owe?"

Phoenix chuckled. "Somehow, I don't see any of us going anywhere anytime soon. You planning to bail on us after you finish ensuring Sadie is safe?"

"Fuck no. Never. You've all agreed to help me get her out of this mess. I'll be here to do the same for each of you."

"It's settled then," Caesar agreed as he rose to his feet. "We're a team. We have six missions coming at us. Looks like Sadie is the first mission." He held out a hand, palm down. "I'm in this for the long haul. Anyone else?"

The other four men stood with an outstretched hand as Rocco entered the circle. They each slapped a hand on top of another hand until they had a pile and then lifted them in a dramatic wave of arms.

Rocco knew one thing for sure. He may have only known these guys for a few hours, but he was in good hands. They were a team. Sadie would be safe as long as they all had her back.

Now, he just needed to find the right time to tell her what he knew and what he planned to do about it. He dreaded that confrontation, but it wasn't going to happen tonight. Tonight, he needed to open his computer and place an order for bedding, books, toys, dolls, games, coloring books, clothes, and whatever other accessories he could think of for a Little girl's playroom. He doubted there was overnight delivery in the middle of New Zealand, but maybe the local shops in town had most of what he needed. He could place an order with them and go pick up everything he needed sometime tomorrow.

Chapter Ten

When her alarm went off the next morning, Sadie groaned as she stretched under her sheets. She was so not a morning person. Dragging herself from the welcoming bed, she jumped in the shower to try to wake up. Leaving the warm water for the cool air filling the bathroom was another tough task.

By the time she finished dressing, it was too late to make something for breakfast. Figuring she'd have an early lunch, Sadie headed downstairs to open the door for the workmen. She'd been a bit hesitant in letting everyone in without IDs or a list of who should be there, but all the workers had focused on their jobs, and she'd had no hint they weren't who they said they were.

Catching herself looking around for one handsome man, Sadie admonished herself. Maybe he'd changed his mind. *I never thought I could become someone's Little so fast. It's just...* "Ridiculous."

"What's ridiculous?" a familiar voice asked from behind her.

"Rocco. Wow! What happened?" she asked, looking at his battered form. Small patches of dirt were scattered over him, and one large swoosh decorated his handsome face.

"Just planting some anchors in the rock cliff to create a pathway for climbers." He looked down at the dirt ground into his T-shirt and grimaced before trying to brush it out. "It looks like I brought half the mountain back with me."

"Oh! Look at your hand!" Sadie grabbed a bunch of tissues and patted them to the slice on his hand.

"Whoa, Little girl. Don't clean up anyone's blood without gloves. What if I had some horrible disease that's spread through bodily fluids?"

She continued her efforts to clean him up. "You don't."

"You don't know that."

Sadie lifted her hand away from the wound. "Okay, you tell me. Do you have something that I can catch?"

"No, I tested clean before I came," he stated with a shrug. "I think it's better. Thanks for mopping me up." Looking around, he asked, "Do you have any bandages here?"

"I should." Turning to look for the first-aid kit she knew she'd inventoried just yesterday, Sadie spied it under a stack of forms. After pulling it out, she opened the top and found two small packets. "Looks like whoever stocked this kit thought kids would be the ones getting hurt. What do you say? Lady bugs or Dinosaurs?"

"I think I'll need both. Let me get this cleaned up first." He turned and walked to the bathroom as Sadie attempted to play it cool and not look at his butt.

When he returned a few minutes later, she carefully placed the ladybugs behind the dinosaur, so it looked like they were chasing the mighty beast. Sadie tried not to giggle as she looked at it. His chuckle made her give up the battle.

Their laughter blended together as his hand cupped her cheek.

"Thank you, Little girl."

He gave her plenty of time to move away or protest, but Sadie didn't move. She didn't breathe. When his lips finally pressed against hers, she couldn't stop her response. Tangling her fingers in handholds of his dusty T-shirt, she clung to him. When his kisses were too light, she slid her hands over his hard chest and wrapped her arms around his neck. She clung to his body, rising on her tiptoes to deepen the kiss.

His groan encouraged her to stroke her tongue over his as his flavor tantalized her. Daring to see how far she could push him, Sadie wiggled her body against his. There was no doubt he was attracted to her. She could feel his cock stiffening against her. When he shifted away, she tried to follow him.

"You are a temptress, Little one," he said softly. "I want you just as much, but here is not the time or place."

Sadie stiffened, remembering they were in the hotel's reception area where anyone could see them. She stepped back and looked down at the black dress she'd worn today. It was covered with the ground-in remnants of his mountain climb. Quickly, she strived to brush off the evidence of her move to seduce him.

Not looking at him, she whispered, "Sorry."

"I'm not."

His enthusiastic response made her look up at him.

His gaze locked with hers. "Can I accompany you into the gardens this evening?"

"I'd love that," she whispered.

"It's a date. I better start the process of getting cleaned up. I'll meet you here at the front desk at seven. Don't leave the building without me." He lifted a brow.

She gasped as it dawned on her that he seemed to know she'd gone to the gardens last night. "I'm an adult, Rocco," she insisted, feeling miffed at his high-handedness on this topic. "I'm perfectly capable of walking outside on my own." She crossed her arms. "And how did you know I went out last night? Were you spying on me?"

"I wasn't spying on you, Little girl," he said sternly. "No one was spying on you, but there are security cameras all over this property to ensure employees and guests are safe at all times."

"Oh." She glanced around, noticing for the first time there were indeed discreet cameras in the corners of the lobby.

He stepped closer. "Don't worry, sweetheart. There are no cameras in your private room. Nor are there cameras in my apartment."

She swallowed at the thought of his apartment. She wondered when he might invite her to see it, which caused her mixed feelings. Were they moving too fast? Should she even be engaging in the idea of getting involved with him at all? She really needed to tell him about her problems if she was going to continue...

Continue what? It was difficult for her to fully accept the possibility that he might really be her Daddy. She'd waffled all morning, worrying she'd imagined their intimate discussion and kiss last night. Now that he was in front of her, it was clear he'd meant everything he'd said. His gaze was locked on hers, and he was studying her intently.

What if she told him about her previous employer and her concerns, and he decided he didn't want to get involved in something so messy?

Rocco reached for her crossed arms and gently pried

them open to ease her hands down. "I know you don't know me very well yet, Sadie, but do you think you could give me the benefit of the doubt for now and not get so defensive and sassy?"

She blew out a breath. "Yes, Sir," she whispered, feeling chagrinned for jumping down his throat.

"Good girl. Now, you're not in trouble for walking in the gardens last night. We hadn't established any boundaries or rules about such things yet, but today is a new day. I don't want you wandering alone outside in the dark while the resort is sparsely populated and so few people are around. It's not safe. If you want to stroll in the gardens at night, you'll ask Daddy to take you, understood?"

She nodded, "Yes, Sir," she whispered again. He had a way of causing her to submit to him and refer to him reverently with just a look. It sent a chill up her spine. Besides, he was probably right. He had no idea there was a possible threat against her because she hadn't told him yet. She needed to do that soon. She would do so tonight.

With an internal sigh, she mentally acknowledged that, if he continued insisting he was her Daddy after she spilled the beans, there was a good chance her freedoms would be curtailed even further. The man had spoken of safety more than once.

"Good girl," he repeated. He gave her one of his winning smiles and leaned in to plant a quick kiss on her lips.

Would she get more of those kisses? Or would that be the last one? She reminded herself that telling him about her problems wasn't her only hurdle. Mr. Kingsley was also standing in their path.

Rocco had said he would speak to their boss, but she doubted he'd had a chance yet, and when he did, there still existed the possibility that she would be fired. Heck, Rocco might get fired, too.

The sound of the front door opening made Sadie blush as she took a step back. She really needed to remember she was at work and stop going all googly-eyed every time Rocco stepped into a room. She wasn't behaving professionally at all.

In fact, she gasped as she jerked her attention to the camera she'd discovered minutes ago. Even knowing someone could be watching her, she'd still kissed Rocco in the lobby. *What's wrong with you?"*

A man strolled into the lobby. "I have a delivery. Do you know where you want me to put it?" he asked as he approached.

Sadie frowned as he got closer. He wasn't holding a package or anything.

Rocco turned toward him. "Is it furniture?"

"Yes," the man confirmed. "I have a new phone here as well for Sadie Miller."

"That's me," Sadie said with a smile. Mr. Kingsley had sent her a work phone as she'd requested.

"I'll help you with the other things," Rocco said. "We can put it here in the lobby. I'll get some other guys to take it upstairs."

The guy nodded. "That would be wonderful. I was worried." He chuckled. "I'm already behind today. When I saw the size of this building, I figured I was going to be here a few hours getting all this up to the fourth floor or something."

Rocco smiled. "Nope. You're off the hook on that." He turned back to Sadie and kissed her cheek. "I'll help unload the truck. We'll talk more later, okay?"

She nodded, wondering what on earth was being delivered. Mr. Kingsley hadn't emailed her about anything else that would arrive like he usually did. Especially an apparently large order.

The delivery guy turned and headed back out the front door.

When Sadie stepped forward to investigate, Rocco shot her a silly smirk. "Don't be nosy, Little girl. I bet you have something else you could be doing."

Her mouth fell open. Nosy? Now, her curiosity was seriously piqued.

Rocco returned to face her and leaned in to whisper in her ear, "Did you want to find out what it feels like to get your bottom spanked already this morning, sweetheart?"

Her breath hitched. "No, Sir," she murmured in response.

"Then I suggest you turn around and let Daddy handle this delivery without snooping. I'll program all of our numbers into this new phone and bring it to you, and I promise you'll find out what everything else is eventually." He leaned back and met her gaze. His eyes were twinkling mischievously.

Which one of them was naughty now?

She decided this odd little game was kind of fun, though, and since he'd said she would get to see the delivery at some point, she would do as she'd been told and go find something else to work on. She kind of liked the idea of surprises. What on earth could possibly be arriving that was large and obviously involved her in some way?

When she didn't move fast enough, Rocco took her shoulders and turned her around before swatting her bottom playfully. "I'll meet you here in the lobby at seven, Sadie."

"Yes, Sir."

As he turned toward the entrance and started walking

away, she very definitely watched his ass. With a much better attitude than she'd had before this encounter with her Daddy, she decided to dive into her list of jobs to finish today. The guests would be coming at the end of the week. She needed to get a move on, checking off the tasks.

Chapter Eleven

It only took about an hour for Rocco and the rest of the team to get all the furniture up to the fifth floor. They dropped unassembled furniture boxes in everyone's spare rooms before heading for Rocco's playroom to help him get everything put together.

He was excited to have this space coming together. Sadie might not be ready to sleep in his bed yet, but he wanted her sleeping in his apartment as soon as possible.

He'd been restless last night after leaving her alone in her studio on the fourth floor. There weren't even other people on the fourth floor. He figured he would have to endure at least a few more nights of separation before she would be ready to agree to move into his apartment, but those nights weren't going to be restful.

After assembling the furniture, Rocco showered and headed into town to pick up the orders he'd placed with a few local merchants. He was beyond pleased with his purchases and had nearly everything in place with time to spare before dinner.

He had a phone call to make first. Luckily, Kingsley had left a contact number for the men to use. Rocco wasn't looking forward to this particular conversation, but it needed to happen.

Hell, he didn't even know where Kingsley was on the planet. No idea of the time zone or the country or anything. All he could do was try to contact him and see what happened.

The phone clicked several times as if it were being transferred through different connections. As he processed that Kingsley had security measures in place for himself as well, the man himself answered, "Rocco Thompson. I was wondering when I might hear from you."

Rocco was taken aback by Kingsley's words. "You were expecting me?"

"Of course. How are you settling in?"

"Fine. Though I'll admit you have all of us a bit on edge with the delivery you arranged for today."

Kingsley chuckled. "I believe in due time you'll all need those spare rooms. Am I wrong?"

Rocco inhaled deeply. "No, you're certainly omniscient. It's unnerving."

"I don't know why. You're not a criminal, and nothing in your past would suggest I should be leery of you. I wouldn't have pulled you into the team and entrusted you with protecting Sadie if I hadn't done a thorough background check on not just you but each and every one of you."

The thought of Kingsley digging so deeply into Rocco's life was unsettling, but knowing he'd done so for every one of the guys was kind of reassuring.

"I know you didn't call just to chat about furniture or your team members."

Rocco cleared his throat. "No. I wanted to make you

77

aware of the fact that Sadie won't just be a job for me. She's—"

"Your Little," Kingsley supplied, cutting Rocco off.

"Yes."

"I assumed that would happen. I won't be standing in your way."

Rocco opened his mouth, hesitated, and then spoke. "Please tell me you're not some sort of matchmaker."

Kingsley chuckled again. "Not exactly. All I did was pick the man I thought best suited for the job of protecting her. The rest is up to you. Surely, you didn't call to get my permission. You don't seem like the sort of man who would ask anyone to grant you permission to claim a Little girl."

"Not at all. I'm calling for Sadie. She's concerned about her job, and I want to be certain you don't have some sort of fraternization policy that would make her feel like her job was in jeopardy."

"Nope. You can reassure Sadie her job is secure. I hired her for two reasons, Rocco. I'm sure you've speculated about my intentions. So before you ask, yes, I knew her life was in danger. As you know, I'm in the business of protecting the innocent. Sadie falls within that category. However, I didn't put her in charge of the front end of things simply out of kindness. She's a hard worker with a good head on her shoulders. She has past hotel experience. She's only been there a few days, and already the operation is running smoother. I would hate to lose her."

Rocco smiled. He agreed with Kingsley's assessment. Sadie was sharp and on the ball. Nothing would get by her.

"However," Kingsley continued, "whether or not she remains in my employment is up to you and her. I won't penalize either of you if the two of you decide it's not in her best interest to continue working for the resort. She will always remain welcome."

Rocco hesitated, once again surprised by his benefactor's words. Was Kingsley suggesting that if Sadie and Rocco entered into a more permanent relationship, Kingsley would understand if she stopped working altogether? That was the only possible inference.

Rocco cleared his throat. "I doubt you'll have to worry about that. Sadie is incredibly conscientious. She isn't likely to want to quit her job and become a full-time Little. I appreciate the sentiment though. I would never get in the way of whatever she decides about her employment. That's up to her. As long as she's healthy, safe, and happy, she will have my support either way—working full-time or not."

It shook Rocco to the core to realize how incredibly serious he was about Sadie and the words he'd just spoken. Saying all of that out loud and knowing he had the support of his boss eased his mind considerably. It also drove home just how invested he was in her.

Sadie Miller was his Little girl in every way. From this day forward, he would do whatever it took to ensure precisely what he'd just promised Kingsley. His top priority was now her health, safety, and happiness.

"Anything else you need to discuss?" Kingsley asked.

"Not at this time."

"Okay. Take care of that Little girl, then. I'll be in touch."

"Thank you."

The call ended, and Rocco inhaled long and slow. That had gone much better than he'd expected. After dinner, he would meet up with Sadie and take her on a walk through the gardens. He would let her know about his conversation with Kingsley, and he hoped she would be able to open up about her problems. He understood perfectly why she had yet to mention a word of her recent past, but tonight, he wanted to lay all the cards on the table.

Rocco suspected part of the reason Sadie hadn't said anything yet was because she had no idea just how much danger she was in. He needed to let her in on that detail. In fact, as unsettled as he was about leaving her in her room on the fourth floor each night, he just might insist she sleep in the playroom he'd spent the day setting up. It wasn't as though it was still an empty room. There were finishing touches to be made, but Rocco wanted Sadie's input for some of the final purchases.

It was with a smile on his face and released tension in his chest that he left his apartment to join the team in the kitchen. He wondered what Sadie was eating for dinner, and part of him wished he'd simply swooped in and demanded she join him and the rest of the team, starting with this meal.

That would have been slightly premature, however. He needed to speak to the other men first and ensure no one minded including her. Their opinions didn't really matter in the long run, but it would be nice if he had their full backing and support.

Chapter Twelve

Sadie paced the lobby while she waited for Rocco to join her. She'd arrived fifteen minutes early because she always liked to be prompt—and because she'd been anxious to see him.

At five minutes before seven—right after she'd glanced at her watch for the tenth time—Rocco appeared.

As usual, he took her breath away with his perfect-fitting jeans, long-sleeved navy Henley, and hiking boots. It seemed the man lived in his hiking boots. It also seemed he had many pairs.

He's a mountaineer, silly. Of course, he has lots of hiking shoes.

His hair was perfectly swept back and his beard recently trimmed. And he was smiling at her like she was the most important person on earth, which made a shiver race down her spine.

"Hey, sweetheart," he said in a sultry tone as he reached her. He wasted no time cupping her face and planting a long, gentle kiss on her lips.

Breathless and wanting more, she whimpered when he ended the kiss.

He winked. "Such a temptress." He took her hand and turned toward the rear of the building. "Let's go out for our stroll before I change my mind and decide to make out with you behind the front desk like a teenager."

She giggled. "That doesn't sound so bad." Then she glanced at the subtle flashing green light in the corner closest to them. "Who has access to those cameras?"

"Magnus is our in-house computer god. He won't tell a soul what he sees that isn't his business. I promise. He's a good guy."

"What about Mr. Kingsley? He installed them, I assume. Do you suppose he might be watching remotely?"

"I think that's unlikely, and even on the off chance he was, I spoke with him a few hours ago to confirm that he won't be disappointed in our union. He reassured me that he's happy for both of us and wanted you to know that you should follow your heart. I'm paraphrasing."

Sadie blew out a relieved breath. "You're sure he doesn't have some sort of policy against workplace romances?"

"Certain." Rocco stared her right in the eye. There was no way he was lying. "Any other concerns?" he asked.

Sadie stiffened. The blood drained from her face as she stood frozen in her spot. She'd given herself several pep talks today, promising herself she would tell him all about her previous job and how she'd come to be here. Still, she hadn't expected to be given such a blatant, wide-open segue so soon into the evening. She'd hoped to be able to stroll through the gardens with him before she brought it up. But there was no way she could put it off any longer.

Shaking, worry eating a hole in her, she licked her lips

and took a deep breath. "Actually, there is something else I need to talk to you about, Rocco."

He smiled. "Okay, sweetheart. Why don't we head out into the garden? The fresh air will help you relax so you can tell Daddy what's on your mind." He leaned in and kissed her cheek. "Also, I'd love it if you'd call me Daddy, at least when we're alone—when you're ready, of course."

"Yeah, well, you might not want me to call you Daddy or Rocco after my confession."

"Confession? That does sound serious."

"Let's go out to the garden," Sadie suggested, wanting the haven the darkness would provide. Plenty of lights illuminated the night, but there were also patches of shadows that would hide her expressions. Rocco could read her so well. Maybe the evening would hamper his Daddy skills.

Daddy skills! A spontaneous giggle escaped her lips at that thought.

"That's a sound I love to hear. Why do I think I'm the one who amused you?" Rocco asked as he opened the door for her.

"Oh, no."

When he looked skeptically at her, Sadie added, "Well, not really. Something just popped into my mind. You know, Daddy related."

"And it was funny?" he probed.

"It was. But it wasn't anything bad. Just that you have Daddy skills."

"I can live with you thinking I'm a good Daddy." Rocco took her hand as they approached the gardens.

"What did you think of Mr. Kingsley?" Sadie tried to change the conversation.

"He's definitely sharp and well-informed. He always seems to be a few steps ahead of me," Rocco shared before turning the conversation back to them. "Tell me about your last boss."

"Talk about being a few steps ahead of someone," Sadie grumbled. "What do you want me to tell you? I lost my last job because I didn't blindly follow directions."

"That must have pissed off the management."

"Who cares? That happened halfway around the world. They can't find me now." She felt Rocco's gaze on her face and tried to keep her expression from giving away how scared she was of Sylvester Pushkin.

"So, you just put a box in the wrong place or something silly?" Rocco asked. "And it cost you your job?"

"It was a bit more serious than that," Sadie admitted.

"The world is a pretty small place if someone is out for vengeance. When we get the resort restored and guests and staff fill the rooms, I'll worry less. But for now, the place is easily accessible. I don't like you sleeping on the fourth floor by yourself," Rocco said.

"I'll have staff members moving in on my floor next week," Sadie rushed to reassure him. She didn't confess that she'd felt much better having the group of men above her last night.

"What would you think about sleeping in my guest room for a few nights until we have more people here full-time? There's a twin bed where you and Edgar could sleep very comfortably."

"I can't just move in with you!" she said, stopping in place.

"You're just swapping rooms for a while to make sure Edgar is safe."

"The other guys will think I'm a...floozy."

"A floozy? I haven't heard that word in forever," Rocco said with a chuckle.

"Don't laugh, Rocco. I don't want people to think ill of me. I need to be able to work with everyone here at the resort," she responded indignantly.

"I know the guys won't consider you a floozy or anything else derogatory if you sleep in my guest bed," Rocco assured her.

"I'm not doing it," she stated firmly, crossing her arms over her chest.

"Then, I want you to take this," he said, holding out a keycard.

"Your keycard?" she asked, automatically reaching out for the device when he held it out.

"This will open the fifth floor from the elevator or the stairwell."

"I've been in the stairwell. I could just climb the steps to your level," she pointed out as she stared at the card in her hand.

"You can, but you won't be able to walk into the fifth floor without this," Rocco explained.

"That's unbelievable security. *You* need this card, though, don't you?"

"No. We're set up so our thumbprints open the door. You take it and put it somewhere safe. When you get to the top floor, you'll know my room. There's a penguin on the door."

"Really? A penguin?" Sadie questioned, looking at him instead of the card.

"What else would let you know that's the door to open?" he asked. "Put that card in your pocket, and when you get to your room tonight, you can stash it somewhere safe."

"I'm never going to use this," she said to make sure he understood.

"You'll have it if you need it."

Sadie slipped it into her pocket and felt safer already. If she needed, she could get to Rocco.

They walked quietly for a few minutes, hand in hand. She liked being with him. His presence scared away all her worries and made her feel secure. After a few minutes, she whispered, "Thank you."

"You're welcome, Little girl."

A yawn surprised her, and she quickly covered her mouth. "Sorry. I had a long day."

"You've been working very hard. An early bedtime would be smart. Do you think you could lie down now to sleep?" he asked.

"Probably, but it's ridiculous to go to bed now."

"It's not ridiculous if you need the sleep," Rocco told her firmly. "Let's go up to your room, and I'll read you more of the story."

"I'd like that," she answered honestly before covering another yawn with her hand.

Rocco led her inside, and they rode the elevator to the fourth floor. She clung to his hand for reassurance, happy that he would take care of her and didn't see tucking her in bed as silly and immature. Rocco seemed perfectly at ease, so she relaxed against the elevator wall next to him.

When the doors opened, she followed him into the hallway, noting that he scanned the area. "Are you expecting bad guys?" she forced herself to ask.

"Would your old boss send someone after you?"

"Oh, yeah. If I was still in his town, there'd be no doubt about that. But he doesn't know where I am. And this far away? I don't think he'll decide I'm worth all that effort to track me down."

"What did you find, Little girl?"

"Some strange accounting practices. Nothing that would

make him chase me halfway around the world," she said quickly as they reached her door. With a flick of her key, she opened it and led him inside.

"It always pays to be careful," Rocco reminded her.

"I will, Dad!" she said sarcastically.

"Daddy to you, Little girl." He eyed her skeptically. "Is there anything else you'd like to tell me?"

She shook her head, not wanting to talk about this anymore. Hopefully, it was all nothing.

"Okay, sweetheart." Rocco pulled her close and turned her around to unzip her sundress.

Sadie inhaled quickly as she realized he meant to undress her this time. His hands smoothed over her shoulders, whisking the light fabric off. It slid down her body, trapping her arms against her waist as it caught on her rounded hips. "Daddy?" she whispered.

"Daddy's just helping, Little girl. I bet it's hard to reach all these fasteners behind your back."

Rocco's fingers traced the lace straps down to the thicker band and unhooked the back of her bra. Sadie tried to reach up to keep the material in place, but her hands were caught in the sleeves of her sundress. Looking over her shoulder, she saw Rocco's gaze was focused on something ahead of her. Following the path of his view, Sadie stared into the mirror on the wall next to her bed. Her partially nude body was reflected in the shiny surface.

As she watched, Rocco glided a hand around her waist and pulled her back against him. She loved the feel of his hard body pressing into hers. His heat and scent surrounded her. He spread his fingers to span her abdomen as if claiming her, and his gaze fixed on hers in the mirror.

"I've dreamed of finding my Little girl for a very long time. You are absolutely lovely, Sadie. Daddy is going to touch you now. Would you like to remain tethered by your clothing? Is that more exciting?" he asked, whispering into her ear.

She nodded, unable to speak. How did he know that, if she was free, she'd feel like she needed to resist? With the material trapping her hands, she couldn't stop him. He could do whatever he wanted to her.

Sadie squeezed her thighs together as he lowered his head to press a kiss onto her shoulder. More followed as he trailed hot kisses along her neck, making her shiver with desire. Her gaze flew back to the mirror as that hand against her stomach shifted upward. His thumb brushed along the bottom of her breast, sending sensations through her body. She could feel herself getting wet.

Leaning back, she arched her chest, pressing her breasts forward. "Please," sneaked through her lips.

"Good girl. Thank you for telling me what you need. That deserves a reward." Rocco cupped her breast fully and brushed that rough thumb over her taut nipple. "I'm sorry my hands aren't as smooth as my Little girl's skin."

"No. I like it," she admitted.

"That pleases me, Little one. Do you like this as well?" His fingers plucked her nipple, tugging it slightly away from her body.

When she gasped in reaction, he repeated the process. His other hand took possession of her other breast. Sadie's gaze was fixed on the mirror as she watched his suntanned hands, battered by his work on the mountain face, caress her body. A grin spread over her lips at the sight of the bandages still clinging to his skin.

"You took good care of me when I was injured. Do you hurt anywhere Daddy needs to make feel good?" he asked, watching her in the mirror.

Biting her lip to keep herself from asking him to touch her there—between her thighs—Sadie lowered her eyelids to block him partially from view. She almost danced with arousal. Couldn't he tell she needed him to stroke her even more intimately?

He released one breast and slid his fingers under the material clinging to her waist. His muscular forearm stretched the fabric tightly around her arms, pushing that shackled feeling even higher. She watched the material move as he explored. His touch tangled in her silky hair. Getting waxed had fallen to the wayside when she'd run away. *Would that put him off?* She stiffened against him.

His mouth opened and closed over her shoulder, biting slightly into her flesh. "Stop thinking," he ordered. "Feel."

Tracing the length of her cleft, Rocco whispered, "You are so wet, Little girl. Are you excited to have Daddy touching you?"

When she didn't answer, he dived closer to her core, separating her pink folds to find sensitive places that responded to his touch. "Are you excited?" he asked, tapping randomly on her clit.

Completely distracted by the unpredictable contact that thrilled her, she answered, "Yes."

"That's my good girl." His fingers brushed over her clit, the rough skin almost too much as he pressed a finger into her tight passage. Almost. Okay, it was perfect.

She gasped as he repeated the motion over and over until she was writhing against him. The sizzling zings of desire filled her body, and she leaned against Rocco's hard frame for support. She could feel his cock rigid against her. He did nothing to sate his own desire but focused on her.

One finger inserted inside her became two, and they stretched her. The small bite of pain mingled with the slight scuffing over that small bundle of nerves. Any lover she'd ever had was erased from her memory as he fingered her.

"Imagine what it will feel like when I'm inside you, Little girl—filling you completely. My cock is eager to taste you," he growled into her ear.

Everything exploded inside her, and she sagged against him. His free hand wrapped around her waist to steady her as his caressing fingers continued to push her orgasm higher. She shook as pleasure filled her to a level she'd never imagined before.

When his fingers slowed their movements, Sadie felt like a melted puddle under an ice cream cone. Her eyes closed, she relied on him to take care of her. Rocco rewarded her with a kiss on that spot at the crook of her neck as he released her zipper completely, allowing the material to drop to the floor.

"So beautiful, Little one. These panties make me smile."

She peeked under her lashes to see him drawing along the edges of her chocolate chip cookie underwear. "I have a bit of a cookie obsession," she whispered.

"Penguins and cookies," he said with a smile. "Time to get into bed. Playtime is over."

Rocco drew her panties down over her thighs and helped her step out of the pile of garments. "Are your PJs under your pillow, Cookie?" he asked with a wink.

She nodded and followed him to the bed. He threw her clothes into the hamper she had by the closet. Sadie smiled. Her Daddy wouldn't ever leave a mess on the floor.

Her Daddy. She repeated that over and over in her mind as he helped her into the soft night garments and guided her into bed. Sadie pulled Edgar close and hugged him tightly as Rocco tucked the covers around her. Her body still buzzed with pleasure from her orgasm. Closing her eyes when he leaned over to kiss her forehead, Sadie wiggled into the most comfortable position.

Her Daddy began to read in his deep voice, and she couldn't keep the corners of her lips from curving up in a smile. If only she could go to sleep like this every night. Maybe she should move into his extra room.

Chapter Thirteen

After pulling on her favorite sundress, Sadie rode the elevator downstairs to her usual position at the front desk. After starting her computer, she opened the front door and allowed all the workers inside. In just the first few days, Sadie had established a procedure for them to sign in at the desk and show her their badges. This morning, she recognized most, but a few new companies were reporting for duty. Unfortunately, two arrived at the same time, and their projects were based on opposite sides of the resort.

To Sadie's delight, Caesar arrived at the desk just as she was trying to figure out what to do. "Hi! I'm glad to see you."

Caesar turned to look behind him before glancing back at her. "Me?"

"Yes. These guys are here to look at the stability of the dock. Could you show them where everything is and answer their questions?" Sadie asked, grinning at the immense man.

Caesar turned to the workmen. "I was on my way down there. I'd love to show you a few things I'm concerned about," he answered, looking at the man in charge.

"I've been told only to listen to her," the dock guy answered as he pointed to Sadie.

Sadie's eyebrows rose. "Caesar is my delegate. What he says is what I agree must be done unless he wants to gold-plate the dock. Then double-check with me," Sadie joked, lending her support to the man chosen to head up water-sports at the resort.

"No gold-plating. It will blind us coming into shore," Caesar said with a laugh. "Let me show you the way."

Satisfied that he would be working with someone with the power to make decisions, the boss and his workmen followed the scuba expert outside.

Sadie turned to the other man standing at the reception desk. "Okay, now remind me of what you need. Something about the helicopter pad?"

"Yes. I've been sent to address the stability of the pad. It was reported to be three degrees off level. That's dangerous," the man answered her.

"Three degrees would make that much difference?" Sadie asked.

"You must not be a pilot, ma'am. Could you show me to the pad so I can take some measurements?"

Something just didn't seem right. That warning voice in the back of her head screamed at her. What was it about this guy that set her radar off? Sadie controlled her expression as she nodded to the stranger. "Of course. Let me call someone to the desk to take my spot so I can show you where it is."

Lifting the house phone, she called Rocco's number.

"Hey, Little girl. You looked so cute sleeping last night."

"Hi, Mr. Thompson. Could you come to the desk to relieve me? There's a workman here that needs to assess the helicopter pad. He says it's been reported to be three degrees off level."

"Three degrees off level. What's that nonsense? Helicopters are made to land on uneven grassy areas," Rocco said, laughing. "And why are you calling me Mr. Thompson, Cookie?"

"I know, sir. It is concerning. Will you be able to assist me at the desk?" Sadie asked, hoping Rocco would get the message that she was spooked.

"On my way. I'll bring Kestrel with me. He'll be concerned about this jerk as well."

"Wonderful, sir. I appreciate your help." Sadie set the receiver back on the phone cradle and looked up with a smile. My replacement will be here in a few minutes. Could I get you a cup of coffee?"

"No, thank you. I have a tight schedule. Now that you know someone is on the way, could we head for the helicopter pad?" he asked, moving toward the open door.

"I'm so sorry. I can't leave the desk unstaffed. It shouldn't be too long," Sadie assured him. To her delight, a large crew of workmen who had been working on the pool piled in through the front door. They streamed inside, walking between her and the newcomer who stood a few feet from the desk.

Hearing the rumble of voices, she looked away from the workmen to see Rocco and Kestrel filling the opposite hallway. Immediately, she felt more secure.

When she turned back to the man who'd been so impatient, she saw him getting into a van at the curb outside. "He's leaving!" she called to Rocco and Kestrel, and they sped up to a run. Bursting through the door, she heard Rocco reciting the license plate. Scrambling for a piece of paper, Sadie tried to write it down, but her mind couldn't hold on to the information.

Rocco

"I don't understand," she whispered as the men approached her.

"That was definitely suspicious. I got the license plate number, and I'll report it to the police, but I don't think we'll get far," Kestrel guessed. "Our odds are better at finding something out about him from Magnus. He's running his picture through facial recognition."

"That entire encounter just didn't feel right," Sadie mentioned as she braced herself against the top of the desk for support.

Rocco immediately circled the desk and wrapped his arm around her waist for support. "I'm glad your radar was on point today."

"A helicopter pad should be level, but three degrees off wouldn't hurt anything." Kestrel frowned. "I wonder what he wanted to do over in that corner of the resort?"

"I don't know. Several cabins sit close to the pad, but that's in the far corner of the grounds," Sadie explained.

"There's a road that runs along the other side of the resort," Kestrel added. "I noticed it when I took the helicopter up for a test flight yesterday."

Rocco grabbed his phone and selected a number. "Magnus, do you have eyes on the road that runs next to the heliport?" Rocco's expression sharpened. "Run the time back on that view. Is there anyone out on the road?" After another pause, he said, "Get us any information you can on that van." Rocco tugged her closer as Sadie started shaking.

"Someone was waiting out there?" she whispered as Kestrel stepped away.

"A van," Rocco said. "Magnus will get us more information."

"I thought they couldn't find me here," she murmured.

"Your old boss?" Rocco probed.

"I...I don't know," she lied. Sadie didn't want to involve him in something dangerous. She hadn't truly believed Sylvester Pushkin would come after her or send someone else. Whatever Pushkin and his men were involved in was more serious than she'd thought. Now, she was scared.

Her mind flew a thousand miles a minute. How could she get out of New Zealand without Pushkin knowing exactly where she was headed? She needed to run. Again. It was the only answer.

Rocco shook her gently. "Stop it." He looked up at Kestrel. "Would you man the desk for Sadie for a few minutes?"

"Of course."

Rocco steered Sadie down the hall into the conference room where the team had met together for the first time. He closed the doors and locked them, appreciating the heavy wood that would muffle anything that happened inside. "You need to tell Daddy everything that happened at your previous job, Sadie."

"I...I don't know what you're talking about. I told you."

"You glossed over most of it, Cookie, and you know it."

She licked her lips, staring at him. It seemed like he knew more than he was letting on. How was that possible? Trembling, she cleared her throat. "You already know how much trouble I'm in, don't you?"

"Yes, but I'll be much better equipped to help you if you tell me every detail in your own words, sweetheart."

She searched his eyes, wondering how he knew so much.

"Would you like to keep lying to Daddy and see what happens?"

"Rocco, don't be ridiculous. I'm sure this is a big misunderstanding, and that van is a total coincidence." However, she knew that wasn't true even as she spoke the words.

"That's two." His phone buzzed, and Rocco looked down at his screen. "Hawking just reported that the fencing separating the resort from the highway that passes it was cut."

"Not over by the helicopter?"

"That's exactly where the barrier was removed. Start talking, Sadie. I can't help you if I don't know what's going on," Rocco told her sternly.

"I'm not sure... Wait! Rocco! What are you doing?" Sadie attempted to squirm away as Rocco lifted her from her feet to carry her to a chair.

When Rocco sat down and plopped her face-down over his lap, she knew exactly what he intended. "You can't spank me." She twisted on his lap to look back to see his stern expression.

"That's exactly what I'm going to do if you don't tell me the truth." His hand landed smartly on her rounded bottom, drawing a gasp from her.

"The next one lands on your bare skin, Cookie."

That wasn't a threat but a promise. Combined with the nickname he'd given her last night, Sadie caved. "Okay. I'll tell you everything," she promised.

A knock on the door made them both look at the heavy wooden barrier. "Rocco, the team's here. Update us," Hawking's deep voice requested.

"This isn't over, Little girl. Everyone needs to hear this as fast as possible. Our private conversation will have to wait until later."

Rocco's tone didn't allow her to misinterpret what he was saying. Her bottom wasn't safe yet. She'd take all the delays she could get. "Okay."

After setting her on her feet, Rocco opened the door and allowed the team to stream inside. He returned to Sadie's side and pulled her to sit on his lap this time. "Good timing. Sadie's going to tell us what's going on."

"You want me to explain everything from the beginning?" she asked in a wavering voice.

"If this attempt is as organized as it appears, you're going to need everyone on the team briefed fully to keep you safe. They won't judge you, Sadie," he promised.

"Okay," she said, taking a deep breath before diving into her story. "My last job didn't end so well. I was hired into management and then placed in accounting without any training. I had a set list of procedures to follow as I documented all the expenditures and profits of the company. Even without knowing what I was doing, I could tell the numbers seemed off. I started working on my own after hours to learn how to handle everything properly. The processes I was told to follow didn't match what the experts said."

"So, you asked your boss?" Rocco prompted.

"Yes. And I was told to follow the guidelines I had been given when I started working."

"Did they threaten you?"

"Well...I guess they didn't...in words. There were two big guys in there that looked at me like predators. I felt menaced."

"So, what did you do?"

"I started a second set of books. I did what they told me to do on the work computer and kept a version of the accounts done the way the experts advised them to be done in a hidden folder on my desktop," she admitted.

Magnus pushed the brim of his hat up and leaned forward. Sadie paused, waiting for him to say something, but he simply signaled her to keep going.

"I know it was stupid. I made notes of where differences were and even made a list of certain names that cropped up a lot. What seemed weird at first became ominous. Then certain words started appearing a lot."

"What words?"

"Things in a different language. I finally looked them up when I saw them repeatedly. When that didn't make sense, I checked a slang dictionary online."

"At work?" Magnus asked.

"No, at home. I didn't enter anything on the computer the boss wouldn't have approved, but I made notes to adjust my secret copy. I assume someone eventually figured out I was sending a second file to my home email," she explained.

"Did they come after you at home?" Rocco asked through visibly gritted teeth.

"No. My computer was gone from my desk at work when I walked in one day. I was told to go pick it up in IT. I snuck out with the garbage men when the doorman barred me from returning to my car for my phone. It was the excuse I used to try to get out of there."

"And when they wouldn't let you leave, you knew something was very wrong," Hawking guessed.

"Yes. I ran to my car as fast as I could and tore out of there. I only stopped at my apartment to grab my computer and...Edgar." She whispered that last word, embarrassed for everyone to hear her. "I left everything else I had behind, stopped at the bank to make a huge withdrawal, and drove out of town. I stayed in a motel for weeks while I applied for jobs, eventually getting this one."

Rocco hugged her. "Good job. I'm so proud of you for making smart decisions—and listening to whatever signaled to you that the man wanting to inspect the helicopter pad wasn't on the up and up."

"Do you think he would've abducted me?" she whispered.

"Probably." Rocco didn't allow her to think about that for too long. He asked, "What kind of clues can you give us about this guy? What color eyes did he have? Any accent?"

"He had mean eyes. The other workmen joke and flirt with me. This guy was totally different." She shivered, remembering how dead his dark eyes had looked.

"Dark eyes?"

"Yes, black. He had blackish hair as well. It looked strange, like an old man who'd dyed his gray hair black, and it ended up looking like he'd used shoe polish. Fake."

"Good. Anything else?"

"He kept one hand in his pocket. You don't think he had a gun, do you?" Sadie gasped.

"I'm sure he had a gun," Hawking stated firmly before adding, "but he was probably holding something else to signal the van."

Glancing from one man to another, Sadie tried to calm her racing pulse. "Where do I go now?"

"You're through running, Sadie," Rocco said, his voice firm. "We're going to track down the threat and take care of it. I'd like to see the emails you sent yourself while working at your last job. It'll help us know how deep your boss's criminal activity is. Meanwhile, we're going to change a few things around here," Rocco announced.

Sadie looked at each man's face. They all held the same resolve. "Okay. I'll have to trust you. Tell me what I need to do."

Chapter Fourteen

By the afternoon, a sign was erected by the front drive, directing all workers and delivery vehicles to the service entrance. Hawking stationed one of the security staff he had already begun to train at that entrance to screen out anyone who didn't seem to belong there. His staff had also contacted all crews already on site that day to update them on the new procedure and to move their vehicles from the entrance.

Sadie looked across the empty lobby and through the front doors to see uninterrupted open space. Changing the flow of workers from the main entrance to the service drive would have happened anyway when the guests arrived. Hawking had simply moved the timeline up.

The panic button in her pocket felt very heavy. Each time she moved, it reminded Sadie that there were bad guys after her. The men had also attached an emergency button to the underside of the desk surface so that anyone on staff could alert them without hesitation. Sadie was updating her training notes for those checking in guests on its presence and when to use it.

Her first crew of trainees was coming in tomorrow. This change would take a huge burden off her shoulders. Sadie had worried about how she would man the desk and take the new staff members on tours to different sections of the resort where they would work. She tried to convince herself that maybe there were simple excuses for everything that had happened today. Her twisting gut told her no.

"Dinner tonight with the guys on our floor, Sadie," Phoenix said as he entered the lobby.

"Oh! I don't want to interrupt everyone's dinner plans," she insisted.

"You're not interrupting. You're joining. We've all settled on having dinner together so we can talk about what's happening and how progress is going," Phoenix said. "You're part of how things are going. You don't want us talking about you, right?"

"No, of course not."

"Then join us for dinner." Phoenix walked over to close and lock the front entrance. "Ready?"

"I'll just go freshen up in my room, and I'll be there in a few minutes," she rushed to assure him, never intending to join the men for dinner.

"Okay. I'll ride up in the elevator with you."

"Are you guys keeping me in sight?" she asked.

"Yes. Besides, we're going in the same direction."

"Up, you mean? I'm stopping at my apartment on the fourth floor," Sadie explained patiently.

"You may wish to come up to the fifth floor now," Phoenix said, obviously avoiding saying something else.

"I'll be there later. I want to finish this training module and print off the new sheets."

"I'll wait with you," he said, propping one hip against the counter and grabbing his phone to type out a message.

Rocco

Sadie jumped a minute later when her phone buzzed next to her. "Hello?"

"I moved all your stuff upstairs into my room," Rocco told her.

"What?"

Phoenix looked at her and said loudly, "Rocco, I think you should come downstairs."

"I think you should come downstairs as well, Rocco," Sadie said sarcastically.

She'd had just about all she could handle today. First, that guy, then having someone guarding her all day long. She was done. It was as if Rocco knew she planned to get in her rental car and head to the airport the first chance she got. Well, she hadn't quite decided to do that yet, but even if she could talk herself into it, Sadie hadn't had a minute alone to dash for the door.

Disconnecting the call, she smacked her phone down on the counter and watched Phoenix wince from the corner of her eye. She knew she wasn't behaving well. Who would? Throwing herself back into her work, she studiously ignored Rocco as he approached.

"Good luck," Phoenix said as he left the two of them alone.

"Sadie."

"Don't Sadie me! You are not the boss of me. I'm not trapped here," she spat.

"I'm only trying to keep you safe, Little girl."

"Don't 'Little girl' me!" Angrier than she'd ever remembered being, Sadie picked up the notebook she'd been putting the updated directions in and lobbed it his way, expecting him to dodge it easily and really be angry when he did. To her surprise, he didn't move.

The binder caught him in the chin, and a thin line of

blood trickled down his neck. Horrified at her behavior, she grabbed a handful of tissues and rushed around the desk, kicking the thick office folder away. Pressing the white tissue to his chin, she apologized, "I'm so sorry, Rocco. Why didn't you duck?"

"You seemed to need to hurt something. Better me than yourself," he said as he wrapped his arms around her waist to pull her close.

Taking the tissues from her hand, he tucked a couple with droplets of blood under the collar of his shirt before wiping her cheeks dry with the clean ones. "You didn't even know you were crying, did you, Cookie?"

"Stop being so nice to me. I just bonked you with a weapon!" she sobbed.

"Seems like you have a lot of feelings to get out. Did throwing that binder help?"

"Yes! Yes, it did," she tried to state firmly, hating it when her voice trembled.

"Come here, Sadie. Let me hold you." He pulled her against his hard chest and held her firmly in place, rocking her rigid body back and forth as he rubbed her back. Slowly, her sobs lessened, and she relaxed against him. "That's my girl."

"Why you'd even want me as your Little girl, I don't know. I'm vicious, and I come with a lot of garbage you don't need," she said as she regained control of her voice.

"Vicious isn't a word I would use to describe you, Sadie. Scared. At your wit's end. Unsure who to trust. Those are all much better phrases for the emotions I suspect are running through you right now."

"Panicked," she added.

"Definitely panicked."

"How do I know I can trust you? Or Mr. Kingsley? Maybe this is all a giant ruse to get rid of me," she suggested, sharing a couple of the million thoughts rattling around her brain as she tried to look self-assured and calm.

"Let me tell you a story. A couple of years ago, I did something pretty naïve. I was tired of my office job, so I became a mountain guide. I heard about a large group offering a ridiculous amount of money to be guided through the peaks. All the more experienced guide companies turned them down, but I volunteered for the job."

"That doesn't sound like a good idea," she murmured as she studied his face. It was etched with emotions, and Rocco looked a decade older than he'd ever appeared.

"If it hadn't been for a team sent by Kingsley to intervene, I would be bones at the bottom of a ravine right now. One of the men gave me a marker and told me it would be called in when I could repay my benefactor for saving my life."

"That's why you're here now?" she whispered.

"Yes. Bad things happen to good people. Sometimes, they're too eager and stupid like I was. Other times, someone's in the wrong place at the wrong time and asks too many questions, like you."

"Are you going to be able to save me?"

"I'm going to do my best, but you have to start working with me and not against me, Little girl."

"Where should I go?" she asked.

"You'll stay here with me. There are six men who will do anything to make sure you're protected, but you can't run. Here, we can control the odds. Out there, too many variables make it hard to protect you. I need you to trust that we are working on this threat day and night. We will put an end to it."

Becca Jameson & Pepper North

She nodded, overwhelmed. "I can't even think."

"I know. You didn't eat lunch, and I suspect you skipped breakfast," he said gently, searching her face.

When she nodded, he added, "Your brain needs fuel to process clearly. So, it's time for dinner. Then a spanking and bed in my guest room."

"A spanking?"

"Don't you think you've earned one today?"

"Yes, but...it's been a really bad day. Phoenix said you moved my stuff upstairs. That pissed me off."

"It didn't. You were already scared to stay in your room on the fourth floor all alone," he pointed out.

She opened her mouth to argue and saw the faint red line on his neck. Nodding, she agreed. "I was already plotting to switch rooms every night so no one could find me."

"How well do you think I would sleep knowing you were unprotected after today?"

She grimaced and guessed, "Badly?"

"Exactly. So, the guys and I moved your things upstairs. It wasn't hard. I refilled your suitcases with the contents of your drawers and closet and grabbed your laundry."

"And Edgar?" she asked quickly.

"And Edgar. He's napping in your bed."

"I overreacted, didn't I?"

"Yes. That's why you'll receive a spanking after dinner."

"All the guys will hear," Sadie said in horror.

"I've already tested it out. The rooms are soundproofed."

She pressed her lips together as she contemplated the punishment. "You could give me a warning."

"Not happening." Rocco nodded at the binder on the floor.

Sitting around the table with the guys felt awkward for about two minutes. When they started their talk-if-you-have-the-serving-spoon thing, Sadie couldn't help but giggle. Thank goodness she'd asked them to start the salad circulating the opposite way around the table. It had taken Kestrel and Phoenix talking in turn for her to pick up on what was happening. She had a feeling they were making more of the new tradition than it really was, but then again, maybe not.

What she appreciated most was that no one seemed intent on bombarding her with more questions right now. They must have silently agreed to let her eat in peace.

"I got the anchors in place on the cliff face today. We might have a few people who wish to rock climb without them, but it's a fairly complex wall. I'll only let the most experienced climbers attempt it after I see that they can handle it," Rocco shared with the group as he filled Sadie's plate before heaping the greens on his.

"We definitely don't want to have to try to rescue some macho guy trying to show off for his girlfriend or boyfriend," Kestrel agreed.

"That's so going to happen," Rocco said with a laugh before handing the salad tongs to Sadie. "Some guys will do anything to show off for someone special."

She already had salad on her plate, so she knew that by handing her the tongs, Rocco was giving her a chance to speak. She stared down at the utensil in her hand for a moment to gather her thoughts before looking at each man, one after another, as she spoke, "I owe you all a huge thank you. I was so busy trying to figure out where to escape to next that I failed to tell you how much I appreciate each of you."

She set the tongs in the bowl with a feeling of relief, realizing that she was actually hungry instead of being sick with worry.

Rocco nudged her affectionately as the others chimed in with their denials that she had anything to apologize for. "It's all understandable, Cookie."

"Damn, we need cookies. Did anyone think of ordering dessert for us?" Caesar demanded.

"There's a cake in the fridge. The chef's trying out new recipes. He's already told me to expect a new one every day for a while." Phoenix grinned. "We even have surveys to fill out."

"Surveys? They better not ask frilly stuff like is the level of vanilla sufficient to support the flavor profile," Magnus growled.

Every person at the table turned to look at him.

"What?"

"Flavor profiles?" Rocco repeated. "Anyone who knows enough to talk all fancy is the official representative of the group to speak to the chef."

"I agree," echoed around the room in deep male voices.

When everyone looked at her, Sadie raised her hands. "I've never purchased vanilla in my life. Don't look at me. The chef already stopped asking my opinion when I asked if we could have smores kits in the cabins."

"Smores? That's a really good idea," Caesar chimed in. "Do we have a gas stove up here?"

"They're going to make those kits happen, aren't they?" Phoenix asked, his brows pulling together in concern.

"Oh, yeah. They thought the ten-year-old-and-under crowd would be very excited by them." Sadie tried to control the smile that threatened to spread over her lips at their eager response.

"Count me into *the flavor profile* of a ten-year-old if it includes smores," Kestrel stated firmly.

The laughter that followed wrapped around Sadie, making her feel like she was one of the group. She stabbed into the beautiful salad Rocco had filled her plate with and ate a large bite as the men continued to chat around her. The delicious flavor bolstered her appetite.

Chapter Fifteen

After dinner, Magnus disappeared. The others didn't seem bothered by his lack of social interaction. Kestrel and Caesar loaded their dirty dishes onto the cart, and Phoenix wheeled it back to the kitchen with Magnus's rating scale. The cake had disappeared in a flash. Sadie hoped it would have a permanent spot on the menu.

She swallowed hard when Rocco took her hand and led her to the door that separated his quarters from the common area. Even though she was nervous about the spanking she knew was coming, she couldn't help but smile at the penguin he had indeed put on his door.

Once they were inside and alone, she cleared her throat nervously. "Rocco, I really don't think you should spank me."

"I know you hope I'll decide you need another chance," he stated evenly.

"I had a traumatic day," she said, trying to sway him.

"Why do you think a Daddy would spank his Little girl?" Rocco probed.

"Punishment."

"Do I look like a violent guy only intent on causing you pain?"

"Oh, no. Of course not!"

"As I explained the other day, Daddies spank their Little girls for different reasons. You can't judge it until you try it, and those tiny swats I gave you earlier in the conference room do not count. Some Littles enjoy being spanked. Leaning over someone's lap with their panties around their ankles is erotic. They like the feel of someone having power over them."

"Until it hurts!" she blurted, squeezing her thighs together as the picture of him holding her bare-bottomed over his hard thighs kindled a fire inside her.

"Even after it hurts. For other Littles, pain is a release. It gives them a reason to cry and offload all the emotions they've kept bottled up inside them."

Sadie clamped her lips closed and refused to confess that she could understand that need. She dropped her gaze to the ground and hoped he'd just get it over with.

"Others feel both a release and an erotic thrill. Unless I am mistaken, I think you fit this third category. You've beaten yourself up over being in this situation. I bet you've asked yourself a million times why you didn't just quit your job and move on when things looked even a bit wacky. How many books have you read about Littles being corrected by their Daddies?"

Lifting her head to look at him in surprise at his abrupt change of topic, she opened her mouth to deny she'd ever read one but found she couldn't lie to him.

"That many, hmm? I think it's time for your spanking. It's time to forgive yourself for what someone else did to you and to feel the release your body needs."

Rocco reached out his powerful hands to grip her hips.

Gently, he turned her around and slowly drew her zipper down the back of her dress. Sadie shivered at the feel of the cool air rushing in to brush over the skin he unveiled as the sides parted. He tugged the short sleeves down her arms and helped the dress fall to the floor. Her bra tumbled soon after, leaving her clad only in her panties.

Wrapping an arm around her waist, Rocco guided her to the large padded ottoman. He took a seat and helped her stretch out over his thighs. She wiggled slightly on his hard muscles, trying to get comfortable, but gave up. There was no way he could be cushy. Sadie bit her lip at the feel of him hooking two fingers into the waistband of her panties and drawing them to her ankles.

Feeling very vulnerable, Sadie knew he could see more of her body than she'd ever considered would be displayed during a spanking. The cool air wafting over her skin between her thighs told her he had to see that she was wet with arousal.

"You're very beautiful, Little girl. Tell me why you're getting this spanking."

"I don't know. Because I was bad?" she wailed, hating the emotion in her voice.

"What did you do that was bad?"

"I didn't come to you for help. Even when I knew you'd be there for me, I didn't want to trust you. I thought I could handle it all on my own."

"Do you need to do everything alone now, Sadie?"

"No," she cried out, feeling the tears starting already. "You'll help me. They'll all help me."

"That's right. It's time for you to learn to accept protection and assistance from others and to stop thinking you've done something wrong to merit these attacks," he said, rubbing over her sensitive skin. "Why didn't you just tell Daddy everything that had happened to you at your previous job instead of glossing over it last night, sweetheart?"

She swallowed. "Because I didn't want to involve you or anyone else. I don't want you to be in danger. Also, maybe, I was a little in denial about the extent of my danger. I was hoping they would just leave me alone."

"From now on, I want you to involve me and my team in everything that happens. Understood?"

"Yes, Sir," she whispered, feeling chagrinned.

"I want you to understand something. I've known about your predicament from the day I arrived. The entire team has, and we're working on this from every angle. We have connections in the States, and we're digging into your former boss's dealings. You won't be a sitting duck here for long, Sadie. We will put an end to this threat."

Sadie sniffled. "Okay." She couldn't imagine how these six men were going to stop her old boss from hunting her down, but she badly wanted to believe they could.

"It's time for Daddy to show you how much I care, Cookie." Without warning, his hand rose and dropped sharply on her skin. The sound of his flesh against hers startled her a fraction of a second before the sting registered.

Sadie tucked her hands under her chest and gritted her teeth. *That hurt.*

The next swat landed on her other butt cheek. She wasn't as startled this time, and maybe it wasn't so bad. By the time he'd delivered five spanks, she was calmer. It burned, but it didn't really hurt. The anticipation had been worse than the actual spanking.

Rocco covered her butt with his palm and gently rubbed it. "You doing okay, sweetheart?"

"I think so." Her voice was kind of weak, but she thought he heard her.

"Not what you expected?"

She shook her head. "No, Sir."

"I'm going to keep going now."

"Okay, Daddy..." Her breath hitched as that word slid from her mouth. Even though she'd let herself think of Rocco as her Daddy, she'd only directly called him Daddy one other time.

His breath hitched, too. "That sounds so nice, Cookie. So nice. Daddy is going to keep spanking you so the icky feelings will go away."

This time when he lifted his palm, she didn't stiffen quite as much. She let her body relax over his knees. Maybe it should have felt strange being completely naked while he was fully dressed, but she wouldn't dwell on that. After all, he'd been the one to undress her.

The fact that her panties were tangled around her ankles intensified every sensation. The balled-up material reminded her she was naked and exposed.

When the next swat landed, she released a moan. It startled her. The vibrations seemed to travel to her pussy. The sensation confused her and grew stronger as he spanked her several more times in that spot, right where her thighs met her butt cheeks.

Rocco stopped again. He trailed his fingers over her heated skin while his other hand spread out over the small of her back. "That's called your sit spot. When Daddy spanks you there, it feels different, doesn't it?"

She whimpered and squirmed, wishing he would stop talking and spank her some more.

He chuckled. "I bet your pussy is soaking wet, isn't it, sweetheart?"

114

She squeezed her thighs together.

"Oh no, Little girl. Spread those knees wide." He pinched her sore bottom to emphasize his words.

She yelped and jerked her legs apart.

"That's better. Keep your ankles as wide as you can, wide enough to pull your panties tight. If your panties fall off your ankles, Daddy will punish you further."

Sadie's toes were on the floor, and she parted them as far as she could, the stretch of her panties around her ankles creating an obscene visual in her mind. Somehow, the panties made the entire act seem humiliating in a way that titillated her and made her pussy even wetter.

Since when do I have a humiliation kink?

"That's my good girl." He rubbed her hot bottom. "I know all kinds of feelings and emotions are going through your head. That's normal. It's your first spanking. Let yourself relax and absorb the sensations. Daddy's got you."

She curled her toes into the carpet, feeling oddly restrained by her panties as if the cotton was tethering her somehow instead of the opposite. She was actually tethering the panties.

Daddy continued his spanking, this time landing each swat higher on her bottom. It burned more in that location, and her pussy didn't get the tingling it craved. She was beginning to understand how there could be different types of spankings.

When Daddy increased the pressure, she relaxed deeper. Somehow, each slap against her skin was becoming more and more cathartic. The bad feelings she'd had all afternoon and evening were slipping from her body.

Rocco's hand shifted back down to that erotic zone, and he swatted her there several times before a moan filled the room. It came from her. It startled her.

A second later, he was no longer spanking her. His hand was between her legs. His fingers slid expertly through her soaked inner lips before he thrust two of them into her.

Sadie lifted her head and moaned long and hard. She'd had no idea she'd been so close to an orgasm. The second Rocco touched her clit, she went off, her entire body pulsing with her release as she jerked and squirmed over his knees.

She lost the traction her toes had had against the floor, and her panties fell off. Somehow that small thing made her breath hitch. As she came down from her high, she twisted her neck to look up at Daddy. "My panties..."

He smiled. "It's okay, sweetheart. You can't be expected to continue maintaining a particular position when Daddy gives you an orgasm." He gently lifted her and turned her around so he could cradle her in his arms.

She sighed against him. Her bottom stung against his jeans, but it was a good kind of pain.

After rubbing her back and kissing her forehead for several minutes, he spoke. "What did you think of your first spanking, sweetheart?"

"Mmm. I can see why people enjoy it. I always wondered. Like you said, it's kind of cathartic."

"It can be, yes. Let's get you some water. It's important to rehydrate after a spanking." He helped her stand and steadied her with his hands on her waist.

She shivered and lifted her arms to cover her chest, feeling exposed.

Rocco wrapped his fingers around her wrists and lowered her hands. "Don't hide from Daddy, Sadie. You're a beautiful Little girl. I love every inch of your body."

"I haven't seen a single inch of yours, Daddy," she pointed out.

He smiled. "You will eventually, Cookie."

"Now?" she asked, glancing down at the front of his jeans where his hard-on was obvious.

"No. Not now. You're too raw from your first spanking to make that decision. Soon, sweetheart. Not tonight."

She sighed.

Daddy rose and took her hand. "Let's get you some water." He led her toward the kitchen area. The apartment had an open-concept design. It was modern and had obviously been redone recently.

She hadn't had a chance to look around when they'd first entered, but now she took in her surroundings. The living room and kitchen were one space. A hallway led toward what she assumed was the bedroom. Were there two bedrooms? She thought she saw a few doors.

"I need clothes, Daddy," she pointed out, trembling.

"We'll get your jammies on soon, sweetheart. Water first."

Rocco opened a cabinet and pulled out a sippy cup, making her eyes widen. There were all kinds of dishes and cups on that shelf in various bold colors. All of them plastic. "Why do you have so many things for Littles?"

He smiled at her as he filled the cup with cold water from the fridge. "I placed several orders in town and went to pick them up yesterday. I have a few surprises for you." He screwed the lid on and handed her the cup. "Come. Let me show you."

Realizing she was extremely thirsty, she took a long drink from the cup as she followed him toward the hallway. There were three doors. He opened the one on the right, and she nearly dropped the cup.

Holding her breath, she stared into the room. *Oh my God.*

"What do you think? I didn't choose the furniture. Kingsley had it delivered."

She jerked her gaze toward Daddy. "All those secret boxes that came yesterday?"

"Yep." He smiled broadly.

She gasped. "Did you say Mr. Kingsley ordered this furniture?"

Rocco nodded. "He's a very perceptive man. Apparently, he already knew the six of us were Daddies before he ever requested our presence at the resort."

Her eyebrows shot upward. "All of you are Daddies?"

He nodded again. "It would seem so."

"That explains why all of you are so protective," she murmured as she stepped farther into the room. The furniture was all white. A daybed, a dresser, a bookshelf, a small table and chairs, and a large rocking chair. "It's like a Little girl's dream room," she whispered.

"I hope so. It's your playroom. I hope you can spend countless hours here relaxing and having fun."

She glanced at the bed. "Am I going to sleep in here?"

He headed for the dresser, opened a drawer, and pulled out a thin white cotton nightgown. As he shook it out and held it up, walking toward her, he said, "For now, until you're ready to sleep with Daddy. I doubt I'll be able to sleep without my arms around you once you've been in my bed, but you can still take naps in here."

Her mind was racing. This was so much to take in.

He held up the nightie. "Arms up."

She automatically lifted her arms for him, gripping the sippy cup as she let her hand go through the sleeve. The nightgown was cut like it would be for a Little girl, with thin straps at the shoulders and a ruffle along the hem, but it was almost sheer and incredibly sexy, like lingerie.

She felt decidedly beautiful in it, and when she lifted her gaze to look at Daddy, she knew she was right. He was holding his breath, eyes filled with lust.

She spun around, letting it flare out to taunt him. The hem barely covered her bottom, so she knew he got a glimpse of her pussy as she twirled.

"Naughty girl," he chided. "Looks like I chose well in the nightie department, though, didn't I?"

She giggled. "Are you sure you don't want to take off your clothes?"

He grabbed her shoulders and turned her around. "Bathroom. Now. Teeth and potty." He gave her sore bottom a swat to usher her forward.

"It's too early for bed yet, Daddy," she grumbled as she headed out of the playroom. She turned back to make sure it hadn't been an illusion. Daddy had decorated the room with several sweet touches. The bedding was black and white. Three penguin stuffies in various sizes sat against the pillow. There was a penguin lamp on the dresser, and a penguin nightlight was plugged into the wall near the door.

"It's not finished. I didn't want to make every decision. You can pick out some special things to make it perfect," he told her before he pointed toward the bathroom.

"Really?" The idea excited her. "I've never had a playroom before. Is it really for me?"

He chuckled. "I only have one Little girl. Of course, it's for you, Sadie. And don't think I've forgotten the fact that you just argued with me about bedtime. Little girls need their sleep. I'd like us to spend some time talking before I tuck you in, but when Daddy says it's time for bed, there will be no arguing." He lifted a brow.

"Yes, Sir." His commanding tone and words made her feel something special deep in her chest. Like he cared. He really cared. He had her best interests at heart. He wouldn't put her to bed just to be mean or assert his authority. He would do so because he knew she needed her sleep.

She gasped as she stepped into the bathroom. It was much larger than she'd expected, with two sinks, a shower, and a separate bathtub. It was modern, like the kitchen. She'd noticed that some parts of this resort had an old-fashioned flare that made it look quaint from days gone by. Still, the important details, like kitchens and bathrooms, the electrical grid, the heating and cooling, the safety features, and the security system were all modern and even somewhat futuristic, in her opinion.

Some of the work on the updates was still happening around them, but most of it had been finished recently. Mr. Baldwin Kingsley III had put a lot of effort into getting this place renovated before he'd brought any of them on board.

"Where does that door lead to?" she asked, pointing to the one on the other side of the bathroom.

"That one connects directly to the master bedroom. There's only one bathroom in each apartment, but guests can access it from the hall." He tapped her nose. "And for Little girls who need to potty when they're in their playroom."

She giggled.

He backed up. "I'll give you privacy to potty and brush your teeth. There's a new toothbrush for you in the holder."

When he left her alone, closing the door with a soft snick, Sadie found herself staring at her entire body in the full-length mirror on the back of the door.

She could hardly recognize herself. She held her arms out and smiled. She really did feel pretty. She could see the outline of her naked body through the material. Her breasts were easily defined and her dark nipples discernable. Daddy had certainly chosen this nightgown well. She wondered what else he had in those drawers. He'd obviously done a lot of shopping.

With a grin and a pep in her step, she hurried to potty and brush her teeth.

Chapter Sixteen

Rocco couldn't stop smiling as he wandered back into the playroom to wait for Sadie. Tonight was going so well. He was pleased with himself. He still wanted to have a serious discussion with her, but he hoped it wouldn't dampen the mood.

He headed for the rocking chair and settled in it before she returned. Then he looked around. The room was still rather sparse. It needed more toys, books, games, and decorations, but he wanted her to choose those things. He wanted her to feel like it was her room, not something he'd thrust upon her. Though judging by the look on her face, he didn't think she had been displeased with the items he'd purchased.

When she came back through the door, his breath hitched. She truly was gorgeous in any outfit—and naked—but the nightie he'd chosen made her look angelic. The light from the hallway filtered through the material, outlining her sexy curves and making his mouth water.

She knew it, too, because she stood in the doorway and

giggled, rocking forward and backward to make the hem sway and tease him.

"Come here, naughty girl," he teased. If his cock got any harder, it would push out of the top of his jeans. He held out a hand.

She rushed toward him as though she couldn't stand another moment of separation. Thank God. He couldn't either.

When he lifted her onto his lap, he intentionally let her nightgown settle around her, not under her sweet bottom.

She winced.

"Sit still, Cookie, so your bottom doesn't hurt against Daddy's jeans." He lifted her and resettled her in just the right spot. "How's that?"

"Good. Thank you, Daddy." She pointed at the bookcase. "You got me books."

"Yes. You told me you had to leave yours behind. I wanted to get you started, but if there's anything missing, you make a list, and Daddy will order them for you."

When she smiled at him, her face lit up so brightly it took his breath away. Then she threw her arms around his neck. "I can't believe this is happening," she murmured.

He rubbed her back and held her just as close. "I can't either, Little girl. But I'm so glad."

When she finally released him, she settled comfortably against him. "I'm a lot of work," she whispered.

He shook his head. "No, you're not. Don't think like that. What happened to you was not your fault. As long as you obey Daddy and the rest of the team, trusting us to make the best decisions for you, you'll be safe. That means no wandering off alone—ever. One of us will always be with you. If it can't be me, it will be another member of the team."

She held his gaze. "You can't follow me everywhere all the time. You all have jobs to do."

"Sadie, our number one job is protecting you. It's what we're here for."

She furrowed her brow. "What do you mean?"

"I mean, the reason Mr. Kingsley hired the six of us was to work together to protect people like you, Sadie. We'll be taking assignments. You're our first assignment."

Her eyes went wide. "How is that possible? You couldn't have known I was in trouble."

"Mr. Kingsley knew, sweetheart," he informed her gently. "We're all learning that he knows a lot of things. He's a very powerful man with lots of connections."

"But...but I thought he hired me because he thought I would be a good reception manager. Are you saying he only hired me because I needed protection?" Tears welled up in her eyes.

"Oh, sweetheart, Mr. Kingsley knows you're the perfect person for the reception manager position. Don't you worry about that. You're an important asset to this resort. Kingsley knows he hit the jackpot when he hired you. Even though it's been many years since you worked in the hotel business, he's well aware of your resume."

She swiped at the tears. "Are you sure? I feel like everyone is just humoring me now."

Rocco's chest tightened at her admission. "No, Cookie. No one is humoring you." He gave her a squeeze. "You've already proven this place is going to run like a well-oiled machine under your supervision. We're all certain of that. In the meantime, we will all be diligently making sure you remain safe."

She looked down at her lap and twisted her fingers together. Her lip quivered. "What about you?"

"What about me, Little girl?" He suspected he knew where this was going, and he didn't like her line of thinking.

"Am I just a job to you? Someone you were hired to protect?" she murmured.

"Sadie..." he said in a warning voice. "Yes, I was assigned to protect you, but you know good and well you mean far more to me than that. You were already my Little girl even before I knew you were in any kind of trouble."

"And you still stayed with me." Tears slid down her cheeks.

"I will always be with you, Cookie."

"Okay."

Rocco rubbed her back for a few minutes, letting that sink in before he smoothed her hair back from her shoulder and lifted her chin. "I want to ask you about something so that I understand you better and know better what your experiences and needs are, okay?"

"Yes, Sir."

"You mentioned that you had a bad Daddy ten years ago. Can you tell me about that, sweetheart?" He rubbed her thighs, hoping his touch would help keep her calm, even if his question might be upsetting.

She shrugged. "I was only twenty then, so I was kind of naïve and new to the lifestyle. I mean, I knew I was Little. I'd known that for a while, but I'd just joined a club, so I wasn't wise to the accepted practices among the age-play crowd."

"That's understandable. Is that where you met him?"

"Yes. His name was Lance. He was older than me. A lot older. So, I stupidly thought that meant he knew things and would treat me right. For a few weeks, he sort of courted me at the club. He treated me like I was special. When he suggested we see each other outside of the club, I agreed."

Rocco was afraid he wouldn't like this next part, but he told himself not to overreact and scare her. *Listen to her.*

Sadie drew in a breath and continued. "He stopped taking me to the club immediately. That should've been a red flag because it kept me from learning more about the things I should've expected from a safe, sane, and consensual age-play relationship. Instead, he brought me to his home on weekends and ordered me around, making me cook and clean for him."

Rocco winced. "That's a domestic submissive, not a Little girl."

"Yeah, well, I didn't quite know that. It took me a while, but I grew tired of serving him. I did some deeper research and realized I'd been duped, and I broke up with him."

"I'm glad you figured it out, Cookie. I'm sorry you went through that, though."

Sadie lifted her gaze and met his. "I don't want you to think I'm permanently damaged or anything from the relationship. I've moved on. I just never met another man I trusted enough to be my Daddy is all. I didn't go back to that club for obvious reasons, and I decided it was easier to practice my kink alone rather than risk finding someone else who could be a real Daddy to me."

Rocco's heart hurt for the Little girl inside Sadie who hadn't ever had a real Daddy, but part of him was grateful she was available to be his at this moment in time, too. He leaned her head against his shoulder and rocked her. "Thank you for sharing that with me, Cookie. I'm sorry you had a bad experience. I'm glad it didn't end worse than it could have. I promise you will never be a domestic servant to me, Little girl. Daddy will be the one taking care of you in this relationship, not the other way around."

She snuggled into his chest and wrapped an arm around

him. After a few minutes, she whispered, "I'm scared, Daddy."

He stiffened and leaned back to look at her. "Of what, sweetheart?"

"Of everything. Of waking up to find out you're not real. Of not being the sort of Little girl you want. Of being able to do my job and keep my Little side separate. Of..." Her breath caught, and a sob escaped. "Of those bad men catching me and taking me away from here so I'll never see you again."

Sadie threw her arms around his neck again and squeezed so tightly she nearly choked him. He held her close and rubbed her back. "Nothing is going to happen to you, Sadie. Daddy is going to make sure of it. As for the rest, in time, you'll know I'm real. Every day from now on, you'll wake up in my apartment. And you never have to worry about being a specific type of Little girl to please me, sweetheart. You are already perfect just the way you are. I fell for you the moment you stepped out of the back room when I arrived."

She gasped and released him. "You did?"

"Of course." He smiled at her shocked face.

Her cheeks turned pink. "I thought you were the handsomest man I'd ever seen. I was nearly tongue-tied."

He chuckled. "Then it was meant to be. And I don't want you to worry about keeping your Little separate. You'll do just fine. If you slip up and call me Daddy sometimes, the guys won't care a bit."

"But I need to hire people, and they aren't going to know about our special relationship."

"That's okay. If you don't want them to know, you'll reserve your Little for when you're alone with me and the guys. If other people find out and they can't respect your lifestyle, then they aren't very good people to have around anyway, are they?"

She sighed. "I guess you're right."

"Any other concerns before I read more of our story and tuck you into bed, Cookie?"

She shook her head. "I don't think so." She spun around. "I think I left my water in the bathroom."

He lifted her from his lap. "How about you run and get it while I open the book on my phone."

"Okay, Daddy."

His heart was in his throat as he watched his Little girl skip from the room. She was lighter on her feet after their deep conversations. He hoped he'd been helpful. All he wanted in the world was for his Little girl to be happy, healthy, and safe.

Chapter Seventeen

Sadie hadn't felt this safe in weeks. Or maybe ever. Tucked into the daybed in her new playroom in Rocco's apartment would make any Little girl feel safe. But when she added the fact that the fifth floor wasn't assessable to the general public and any intruder would have to get past six large, growly Daddies to get to her, she breathed easier.

She knew she was supposed to be asleep. After her Daddy had read chapter two to her until she couldn't hold her eyes open, he'd tucked Edgar and one of the new penguins under the covers with her and kissed her forehead before tiptoeing from the room.

Sadie had fallen asleep with a smile and was still smiling as she woke up. The problem was that it was still very dark outside. The only light was coming from the penguin night light.

She had no idea what time it was because there was no clock, and she must have left her phone in the kitchen. The door to her room was open several inches. Daddy hadn't shut it all the way. That fact added to her cozy cocoon.

Snuggling both her penguins against her chest, she luxuriated in the feel of the expensive sheets that smelled so good. Whatever Daddy had used to wash them had left a very pleasant scent.

She closed her eyes and tried to go back to sleep, but her mind wouldn't stop wandering to all the events of the previous days. So much had happened since she'd arrived in New Zealand. It was hard to process it all.

Had she really met her Daddy? She wanted to believe it was true. After all, she was in his apartment, and he'd told her she would be staying here from now on.

He'd given her two amazing orgasms, too, and she hadn't even seen him naked. She intended to rectify that situation first thing in the morning. Was it almost morning?

Suddenly, a loud, piercing noise made her bolt upright in bed. It was so obnoxious that she covered her ears. It took her a few seconds to realize it was an alarm. Like a fire alarm.

"Sadie?" She could barely hear Rocco calling her name over the disturbing dissonance, but in moments he was sitting next to her, pulling her into his arms. "You okay?" he shouted.

She nodded, keeping her hands over her ears.

He scooped her up, tugged the sheet off her bed, and wrapped her in it before stepping out of the playroom, through the living room, and out into the corridor.

The rest of the men were all coming out of their apartments.

"Is it a fire alarm?" Rocco yelled over the din.

Magnus shook his head. "Security system. There's a breach somewhere. Basement. Now." He ran past everyone toward the elevators and stairs.

Rocco gripped Sadie close as he followed the rest of the men behind Magnus.

Sadie might have argued that she could have walked, but

then she remembered what she was wearing and pursed her lips, holding on to her Daddy's neck instead to brace herself and make his journey less difficult.

It was probably only thirty seconds before the seven of them emerged into the basement.

As the last one through the door, Rocco turned and pulled it shut before throwing a deadbolt and a giant iron bar over the thick steel door.

Sadie was trembling, eyes wide. She'd never been in the basement. She hadn't even known it existed. It was huge and looked like some kind of command center for the CIA or the FBI, with all the equipment, flashing lights, and computers.

Rocco deposited her in the corner of a giant sectional— the biggest piece of furniture she'd ever seen in her life, big enough to hold ten people or more. After making sure the sheet totally covered her, he kissed her forehead. "Don't move. You're safe in here."

She barely had time to nod before he ran toward the computer bank with the other men. They all leaned around Magnus, who had taken a seat in front of the most impressive expanse of monitors and electronics she couldn't even recognize. He looked like he was at the helm of a futuristic spaceship.

Sadie didn't move. For one thing, Daddy had told her not to, but she wasn't sure if she could, even if she wanted to. She was wrapped up like a burrito, which was probably a good thing. If anyone besides Rocco saw her in the lingerie she was wearing, she would turn ten shades of red.

She also realized she was still hugging the two penguins to her chest and was grateful. They were comforting. She at least managed to wiggle Edgar up so she could whisper in his ear, "It's okay. We're safe. Daddy said so."

Edgar seemed to believe her because he slid back down

under the sheet a moment later as if not wanting his sleep disturbed. She couldn't blame him. She wished she were still sleeping, too.

At least the sirens weren't as loud down here. The thick steel door muted the sound. There were, however, flashing red lights in the corners of the room that would alert anyone of a problem, probably even if they were asleep.

"Can you back up the footage?" Phoenix shouted, leaning over Magnus's chair.

"Working on it," Magnus said as he clicked away at the keyboard. Finally, the alarm stopped blaring, and the lights stopped flashing.

A dozen screens were lit up, and Sadie quickly realized they were each showing the view of a different section of the property where there were cameras.

"Fuck. Whoever it is took out the camera on the east side of the building," Magnus grumbled. "Must have done it with a long-range rifle. The men who came earlier today probably scoped out the cameras, trying to find a way in."

Sadie shuddered. She was the cause of all this trouble. She'd brought it here. Why would Mr. Kingsley even keep her? He had every right to fire her and kick her off the property. Especially since she hadn't told him about the potential trouble she was in.

Granted, Sadie hadn't imagined this much of a problem following her around the globe. Why couldn't Sylvester Pushkin just leave her alone?

Even though she'd noticed discrepancies in the books and had made copies to protect herself, she hadn't had any way of knowing how important her discovery could have been. Obviously, it was huge, or bad men wouldn't have followed her all the way to New Zealand.

"Are any of the entrances breached? Windows? Doors?" Rocco asked.

"Doesn't appear that way," Magnus responded. "I see no evidence of any entry point being compromised."

"Why would someone shoot out the camera if they weren't going to approach and enter?" Kestrel asked.

Rocco straightened to his full height and ran a hand through his hair. "It was a test. They wanted to know how secure the building was."

"Well, they know now, and we know they have guns despite New Zealand's gun ban," Caesar grumbled. "What time is it?"

"Five," Hawking stated.

Magnus pointed at one of the screens. "The camera I was using to spot their van earlier is also down. They probably hit both of them at once. I bet they have their vehicle at that same location on the road just outside of the property."

Rocco headed for a closet along one wall of the large living. He opened it to reveal rows and rows of various types of clothing. Most of it looked like it was intended for cold weather.

Sadie watched, thinking maybe he was looking for a T-shirt or something since all he had on were his sleep pants. He grabbed something and turned to head toward her.

Rocco settled beside her on the couch, blocking her from the others before tugging the sheet away. "Lift your arms, sweetheart."

She immediately did as she was told, grateful when a huge thick sweatshirt slid down her body. She lifted her bottom to pull it farther down, almost to her knees.

Rocco chuckled as he rolled up first one sleeve and then the other far enough to let her hands stick out. "There." He kissed her forehead again. "Guess Daddy better get you a long, thick robe and keep it next to the bed in case anything like this ever happens again."

She couldn't believe how calm he was.

Hawking suddenly came into view and reached forward, holding out a sippy cup of water. "Thought you might be thirsty, Sadie."

"Thank you," she murmured, a bit shaken by the fact that everyone in the room knew she was Little.

"Where'd you find that?" Rocco asked with a laugh.

Hawking shrugged. "The kitchen is so well stocked it has damn near anything a person could want. Found a drawer of sippy cups, plastic plates, and bowls."

"Once again, Mr. Kingsley proves himself to be uber-prepared and all-knowing."

Sadie took a long drink of the cool water. "Are you sure we're safe in here?" She glanced around, continuing without waiting for an answer. "I didn't know this basement even existed."

"Yep. It's our command center, as you can tell. We all have regular jobs with the resort, but this basement is where we'll deal with threats that get thrown at us," Rocco stated.

"Does that keycard you gave me work for this room, too?"

He shook his head. "No. It only works for the top floor. I'll have to speak to Magnus, and perhaps Kingsley, about getting you clearance to enter the basement. I don't like the idea of you not having a safe place to flee in an emergency."

Hawking, still standing close by, nodded. "I agree. If I had a Little girl, I'd want her to have access to this basement."

When the others trickled closer, Hawking turned to them. "I'm going to go investigate." He nodded toward another closet door next to the one where Rocco had pulled out the sweatshirt. "Now, we know why Kingsley outfitted this bunker of sorts with state-of-the-art munitions."

Sadie sat up straighter, holding her breath as she watched him stride across the room. He had obviously taken a few seconds to put some clothes on before descending to the basement because he wore jeans and a black, long-sleeved shirt. The others were all dressed like Rocco, mostly in sleep pants, either barefoot or with slippers.

When Hawking opened the second closet, Sadie gasped. It held a full arsenal. She'd noticed he'd used his thumb to open the closet. Thank God not just anyone could get into it.

As he pulled out several pieces and strapped them onto his body, she wrapped her arms around herself and shuddered.

Phoenix joined Hawking. "I'll go with you." He rustled through piles of jeans in the open clothes closet until he was satisfied with the size, shrugged into the dark pants and a dark shirt, and snagged a pair of boots next. After handing the first pair to Hawking, he grabbed a second.

"You a good shot?" Hawking asked.

Phoenix smirked. "My father was Army long before I was. He had me at the range by the time I could stand." Phoenix grabbed a handgun and tucked it into a holster, which he stretched across his chest. "Ready."

Magnus strode toward them from the bank of computers. He handed them each an earpiece. "Put these on. I'll watch from every angle and let you know if anything is amiss."

Hawking nodded as he stuck the small device in his ear. "Thanks."

Phoenix did the same. "First thing as soon as the sun comes up, I'll fix the cameras. For now, we just want to ensure whoever took them both out is long gone."

"Hallway is clear," Magnus announced as he returned to the computers.

Sadie stood and wandered closer, mesmerized by the high-tech equipment. She held her two penguins close to her chest with one arm and the sippy cup with the other.

In any other universe, she would have been mortified to expose her Little to other people. She would never have left her room with her stuffies or used a sippy cup in front of anyone. But she was living in a new universe. A safe space. A place where not one single person in the room was looking at her as if she were an alien. In fact, they'd all smiled at her, and Hawking had even brought her the sippy cup.

As soon as Phoenix and Hawking were outside, they showed up on one of the monitors.

Rocco stood behind Sadie, his hands on her shoulders. She was grateful he didn't make her sit back down. She wanted to watch. After all, this trouble was her fault. She didn't want to be left out.

Kestrel took a seat near Sadie, where he could see the monitors, too, but he turned toward her and pointed at the penguins. "Who are your friends, Sadie?"

Her cheeks heated, and she bit her lip, but his expression was serious, so she released her lip and turned her childhood penguin around. "This is Edgar. He's been with me forever."

"And this other fellow?" Kestrel pointed to the new penguin. "I bet your Daddy got him for you, huh? What's his name?"

Sadie shrugged. "He doesn't have a name yet." She felt terrible for not naming the new penguin. He wasn't the only new friend she had either. There were three of them. But this medium-sized one had been just the right size for her to hold at night.

Caesar gasped from the other side of Magnus, but when

Sadie glanced at him, she found he was grinning. "You better give that little guy a name soon."

She giggled. They were all trying to keep her occupied so she wouldn't have to think about the security breach. She knew that, and she appreciated it.

Rocco rubbed her shoulders. "We'll have to come up with a few new names for new stuffies, huh, sweetheart?"

She nodded and leaned back against him.

Hawking turned toward a camera in another zone and gave a thumbs-up before both men headed back toward the main building. Within minutes, they were in the safe room.

Hawking wiped his shoes on the mat inside the door. "No sign of anything in the area. I'd say they came to test their theory about the cameras and then took off. They'll be holed up somewhere regrouping and trying to figure out what to do next now that they know they won't get to Sadie without an all-out war."

Sadie felt like the floor was yanked out from under her as she let herself fully acknowledge the danger she was in and had brought to everyone living here. "I'm sorry," she murmured, fighting back tears. "It's all my fault."

Rocco rounded to squat down in front of her. "Sweetheart, we've talked about this. You know that's not true. You didn't ask for these men to come after you, and you did nothing wrong. Sometimes, bad people do bad things. You're not responsible."

She sniffled, trying to believe him.

"I think it's safe to go back upstairs," Magnus declared. "I'd never be able to go back to sleep, so I'll stay down here and monitor things."

Rocco turned toward him. "I'll take Sadie up and help her get back to sleep. Though I think we need to set up a schedule to monitor the cameras around the clock for the time being."

"I agree," Phoenix added. "At least until we put an end to this particular threat."

Everyone nodded their agreement, and Sadie felt both relieved and chagrined once again. No matter what anyone said to console her, she had indeed brought this problem to Danger Bluff, and she felt sorry for her actions.

Chapter Eighteen

After snagging Sadie's sheet from the couch, he lifted her into his arms and carried her out of the safe room. He headed straight for the elevator. No way would he have risked coming down the elevator while the alarm had been going off, but now that the threat was contained, he didn't fear getting in the elevator to return to the top floor.

"You don't have to carry me," Sadie protested.

He snuggled her against him. "Cookie, I can't stand the idea of putting you down. Humor Daddy, okay?"

She giggled, a sound he loved. "I don't want you to stop touching me either," she admitted, warming his heart.

As soon as the elevator doors opened, he headed straight for his apartment, through the open space, and into her playroom. He sat on the edge of her bed and pulled the huge sweatshirt over her head to toss it aside. "We're definitely going to need to get you a robe," he repeated as he straightened the straps of her nightie. "Either that, or I'll need to start dressing you in footed pajamas in case anyone sees you."

She giggled and shook her head. "No way, Daddy. I'd get

too hot." She looked him in the eyes and set her hands on his shoulders. "Besides, I like how you look at me in this night-gown. I hope you got more of them."

He grinned as he grabbed her hips. "You bet I did. Two others. One is pale pink. One is pale yellow. I'll get five more in the morning."

She laughed. "Maybe you could get matching panties?" she suggested as she squeezed her legs together.

He shook his head. "Not a chance. No panties at night. Daddy is going to want access to his sweet pussy." He slid his hands below the hem of the nightie and up to cup her lower cheeks. "Is your bottom sore from my spanking?"

"No, Sir."

His heart skipped a beat. That happened every time she called him Sir. After another squeeze against her soft skin, he released her. "Let's get you back in bed. You haven't had enough sleep."

She shook her head. "I don't want to go back to bed, Daddy, at least not my bed. How about if I come to *your* bed?"

He held her gaze, wondering if she understood where his mind went at such a suggestion.

She flattened her palms on his chest and cocked her head to one side. "Please, will you take me to your room? I want to be closer to you."

He licked his lips. "How close, sweetheart?"

"All the way close. Like, without the nightie or your pants. Inside me close."

"I've been inside you, Cookie, and I easily did so with my pants on." He was pushing her, but he needed her to spell it out if she was ready to make love to him.

She shook her head again. "Not with your fingers, Daddy. With your cock."

He groaned at her use of the vulgar word as said appendage jumped fully to attention. "Are you sure?" She nodded. "Positive." She glanced at the bed he sat on. "This bed is very cozy, and I love it, but I was lonely in here without you. Can I please use it only for naps and maybe to sit on to read?"

Rocco lifted her off the floor as he stood. "Wrap your legs around me, sweetheart." He was already on the move toward his bedroom as she obeyed him. He didn't waste time, either. He took as few strides as possible to reach his bed, and then he climbed up on his hands and knees with her still clinging to him like a monkey.

She giggled as he dropped the two of them onto the mattress, cupping her face and taking her lips. Her giggle immediately switched to a moan that vibrated through him and made his cock jerk against her.

After kissing her senseless until they were both panting, he released her lips to look down at her. His sweet girl's legs were so tight around him that he was well aware of her heated wet pussy against his sleep pants. "This is why I'm not buying you any panties for nighttime."

She whimpered as she finally let go of his neck, letting her hands fall alongside her head. Her hair flared out around her, making her look ethereal. Her cheeks were pink, and when she licked her swollen lips, he groaned.

After glancing at her chest, he knew he needed some time worshipping those pretty buds he'd admired. He hadn't had a chance to give them the attention they deserved, so he slid down her body, kissing a path from her neck to her breasts.

Sadie kept her legs around him, although they were around his chest now, as he dropped his mouth to one of her nipples and sucked it through the thin material of her nightie. He growled again as he released the first one, needing to switch to the other. "I'm not sure I'm going to let you sleep in these nighties either, Cookie. They're so very sexy when you're walking around in them, but now this flimsy material is in Daddy's way."

She arched her chest, reached down to grab the hem that had bunched around her waist, and tugged the thin night-gown over her head.

Rocco smiled. "Thank you. Much better." He latched on to her second nipple without a barrier, sucking, licking, and flicking it with his tongue until she writhed beneath him.

He loved the way she dug her blunt nails into his back and how she seemed to think she could keep him where she wanted with her ankles connected at his back.

Rocco wasn't going to be hindered by her tiny legs, though. He released her nipple with a pop and eased himself farther down her body. He kissed her belly before moving lower. Without giving her time to think, he buried his face between her legs and sucked her clit.

"Daddy!" she cried out. "Oh, God."

Yeah. That's exactly what he wanted to hear.

Her legs finally lost their grip on his back and fell open.

Rocco smoothed his hands up her inner thighs and held them wide, keeping her from squirming away from his mouth.

She whimpered and wiggled as if trying to free herself. "Daddy..." Between the tone of her voice, the way she was panting, and the tremble in her legs, he knew she was close. He thrust his tongue into her channel. Damn, she was tight, as though she hadn't been with a man in a while. He was going to stretch her when he first entered her. He hoped it wouldn't be too uncomfortable.

"Please..." she begged, "I need..."

He drew her clit between his lips and flicked his tongue

over it rapidly. That was all she needed. A moment later, her body convulsed beneath him, and she cried out her release.

Rocco continued to kiss her pussy, loving the scent and taste of her, until she settled.

She was panting, a huge smile on her face, when he lifted his head. "More, Daddy. Take your pants off."

He wiped his lips on the sheet before shoving off the side of the bed to drop his sleep pants. Afterward, he opened the drawer on his nightstand to snag a condom. Thank goodness he'd had the forethought to stop by a chemist when he'd been in town. He certainly hadn't come to New Zealand with thoughts of finding the perfect Little girl and taking her to his bed.

"Hurry, Daddy," she insisted while he rolled the condom down his length.

He climbed back over her, his knees between hers, his hands on either side of her body, not touching her. "So impatient," he teased.

She nodded. "Need you."

"You're sure? There will be no letting you go for any reason after Daddy has been inside you. No silently packing your things as if you might sneak away at night because you have some misplaced desire to protect me from the fools after you." He lifted a brow.

She gasped. "You knew I was thinking of doing that?"

He nodded. "Daddies know all kinds of things."

She reached for him. "I won't run, Daddy. Please make love to me. I need to feel you inside me. I need to feel closer to you. Enveloped by you."

He dropped his hips and thrust all the way into her without another moment's hesitation.

Sadie cried out, arching her chest clear off the bed as she grabbed his hips. "Oh..."

Rocco couldn't move. He was afraid if he did, he would come instantly. She was so tight around him and so damn sweet. He'd known she was his Little girl almost from the first moment he'd set eyes on her, but he'd never expected this.

This connection was so much more intense than he could have anticipated. Emotions rushed to the forefront, consuming him, making him want to stay inside her forever.

He wouldn't be able to remain in her tight channel for two minutes. As soon as he moved, he would have to grit his teeth to keep from coming.

"Daddy..." His Little girl bucked her hips, trying to get him to give her more. She was so gorgeous, spread out on his bed. She was his life. His world. His everything. If anything happened to her...

He cut off that negative thought and met her gaze, easing out almost all the way before thrusting back into her. So tight. So hot. So wet.

There was no way he could hold himself up with one elbow right now, not with how mesmerized he was. His arms shook with his need to let go and come inside her.

He wanted her to join him, though. "Reach between us, sweetheart. Rub your clit for Daddy."

Her eyes went wide.

"Do it, Cookie. Daddy's not going to continue until your fingers are working your clit. I want you to come with Daddy."

She released his hip with one hand and eased it between their torsos. He knew the instant she made contact because her breath hitched and her eyes rolled back.

Sexiest thing he'd ever seen. "Now, Sadie. Rub harder. Come around Daddy's cock."

She tipped her head back, her mouth falling open, her

back arching off the bed to raise her gorgeous breasts. And then she screamed.

That was all he needed. Rocco picked up the pace, thrusting in and out of her without concern. His Little girl had reached her peak. That had been all that mattered. He could grasp onto his own slice of heaven now.

And he did. When his orgasm consumed him, it affected his entire body and his mind. There was nothing else in the universe except Sadie.

Chapter Nineteen

Sadie was still trying to catch her breath, even after her Daddy had left the room to dispose of the condom. Even after he'd returned and gently wiped her pussy with a warm washcloth. Even after he'd crawled back onto the bed, arranged her so he could spoon her, and pulled the covers over them.

His fingers trailed up and down her arm, causing goosebumps. He kissed her neck and shoulder over and over.

"Thank you, Daddy," she murmured.

He chuckled. "You're thanking me for sex?"

"Yes. It was amazing. I want you to know I appreciated it, so you'll do it again." She twisted to look at him. "When can we do it again?" She didn't care that she sounded eager.

He laughed. "Aren't you sore? You were so tight."

She shook her head. "No. It felt amazing. Perfect. Life-affirming."

He smiled. "That good, huh?"

She gasped and twisted farther to more fully meet his gaze. "Are you making fun of me?"

"Never, Cookie. That was the best sex of my life, and do

Rocco

you know why?"

She didn't. "No."

"Because I've never had sex with my perfect life partner."

She smiled and snuggled in closer, letting her face relax against the pillow. "That sounds so nice." She sighed contentedly.

After long moments of silence, she knew she needed to snap back to reality. "Do you think I'm safe here?"

"Yes, sweetheart. Safer than anywhere else on Earth. No one can get to you here. Did you not see how secure that basement is? And this top floor is damn safe, too. The outside of the building isn't conducive to scaling. Someone would have to repel down from the roof to get to these windows."

She gasped. "What if they do?" Her heart rate picked up.

"Magnus would catch them before they could ever get that close to the building."

"But Magnus can't watch the monitors twenty-four-seven. The six of you can't manage that alone. There will be times when—"

Rocco cut her off with a finger to her lips. "The system has a trigger. It will alert Magnus that something is amiss even if he's not watching."

"Did it do that tonight?"

"I'm sure it did, but the trigger would've been at the same time the alarms went off because a shot to the outdoor camera is what brought the alert."

"Oh..." She was shaking, though. "What if..."

Rocco grabbed her fingers and squeezed them between her breasts. "You let Daddy and the others worry about all the 'what ifs,' okay? I don't want you to worry. As long as you stay inside this building, you can go about your day, doing your job. If you need to go outside for any reason, you let Daddy know, and I'll take you."

147

"What if there had been guests here? What if those bad men keep coming even after we open? That would give the resort a horrible reputation, and then people wouldn't come here for vacation, and Danger Bluff Mountain Resort would be ruined and—"

"Sadie..." he warned, cutting her off again. "I don't think these guys will still be in the country when the resort officially opens for business. They're obviously determined, which means they're not going to give up and lie low somewhere for very long. They will make their next move sooner rather than later, and everyone will be ready."

"Okay," she murmured, though she wasn't sure she believed him. It all seemed so surreal. So many things had happened in just a few days. She'd gone from being homeless and jobless in the United States to having her dream job in New Zealand, meeting the perfect Daddy, and moving in with him.

Surely her luck couldn't hold out much longer. The universe wasn't nearly that kind to her. Some people didn't get their happily ever after, and Sadie was struggling to believe it could be possible for her.

The truth was it was easier to remind herself this could all go up in smoke in a heartbeat than let herself think she could have everything.

"Are you sure it wouldn't be better for everyone if I left New Zealand?"

"Positive, Cookie. That's not going to happen." He held her tighter. "This is where you belong. This country, this resort, this room, this bed, these arms."

An alarm went off, and for a moment, Sadie thought it was happening again. She jerked in Rocco's arms, her breath catching in her lungs.

"It's just my phone, sweetheart." Rocco rolled away from

her for a moment, and the noise stopped. "It's time for me to get up. Why don't I tuck you into my bed so you can sleep for a while longer?"

She shook her head and rolled to her back. "No. I need to get up, too. I have lists of things that need to get done before the resort can officially open. I can't stay in bed all day."

"Okay, but after lunch I want you to go down for a nap, understood? I won't accept any excuses."

She nodded. That seemed unreasonable and probably wouldn't fit in with her schedule, but if it made him happy right now, she would agree to it.

"Sadie..." he said in a warning voice. "You have a mischievous look in your eyes that says you're humoring Daddy. That will never go well for you."

She grinned and shrugged her shoulders. "If I'm naughty, will you bring me up here and spank me?"

He groaned. "Sweetheart, if you're so naughty that you manipulate your Daddy into getting what you want, I'll do much more than just spank you, and I can assure you an orgasm will not follow my punishment."

She gave him a fake pout, sticking her bottom lip out. "Darn."

He chuckled before rolling away from her and off the bed. He reached out a hand. "Let's shower."

She sat up quickly and scooted toward him. She hadn't gotten to see all of him for more than a few seconds before he'd rolled on the condom and climbed between her legs.

Damn, he was handsome. Every inch of him. His cock was still hard and standing out. His chest was broad, his pecs firm; the sprinkling of hair on his body made him even more attractive.

She let her gaze slide up and down his frame until he snagged her hand. "Shower, naughty girl. Now."

"Are you going to shower with me?" she pleaded.

He groaned as they entered the bathroom. He released her to turn on the water. "Yes, but you're going to face the wall while I wash you, and then I'm going to wrap you in a towel and send you to the closet in your playroom to get dressed for work."

"That's no fun," she said, adding an intentional whine to her voice. She hardly knew this side of herself. Whining? Begging? Stalling? This Sadie was new, but she thought she liked her. She was fun and playful, with a naturally connecting personality that always enabled her to make friends easily. Perhaps she would think of ways to get into trouble just to see what would happen.

Daddy had said lots of Little girls misbehaved because they enjoyed having their bottoms peppered. It had seemed silly to her at the time, but now that she thought about it, maybe it wasn't a bad idea.

As Daddy guided her into the shower and under the spray, angling her so she faced the wall, she thought of little ways she could misbehave to taunt him. Maybe that would take her mind off her problems. Instead of worrying about the bad men who were after her all day, she could plot future naughty behavior.

Yep. That's what she would do. It would be fun. At least she thought so.

"Sadie..." Daddy said in a warning voice as he rubbed shampoo into her hair. "Whatever you're thinking, wipe it from your mind, Little girl. You'll be over Daddy's knees before breakfast and spend the day with a very sore bottom if you don't adjust your focus."

She giggled and looked over her shoulder. "Maybe I feel kind of naughty, Daddy."

Chapter Twenty

After sneaking a look around to make sure no one could see her, Sadie rubbed her sore bottom. It turned out plucking soggy cereal out of your bowl and decorating the table with corn flake snowmen was not acceptable in her Daddy's eyes. She'd only flicked one small flake toward him. It could have missed.

He'd flipped her over his lap and yanked up her sundress so fast she hadn't even had time to come up with an excuse. Okay, so she had tried to push his limits to see where the boundary was. Sadie had found it. *That's for sure*, she thought as she smoothed her sundress over her stinging derriere.

She felt her lips curve into a grin. It had been so much fun, though.

"That's a guilty smile if I've ever seen one," Hawking said, coming through the front door.

"Oh, I just thought of a funny joke," she said quickly. When he opened his mouth, she knew he was going to ask her to tell it. "It's a girl joke. You won't think it's funny."

"Gotcha. I'm coming to check on the applicants for the security positions."

"The first guy just checked in. I put him in the conference room where you all first met. How would you like me to handle the next applicants?" she asked.

"Just take their names and have them wait in the lobby. I'll be able to tell if they're right in a few seconds," Hawking assured her.

"Perfect."

"If you have any trouble, hit the panic button or send me a text," he reminded her.

"Go interview your guy. No one is going to try to get me again this morning."

The look Hawking gave her sent a shiver down her spine. Maybe she shouldn't be so comfortable at the reception desk.

For the next hour, in addition to the buff guys who trailed in to talk to Hawking, Sadie enjoyed seeing some very fit women apply as well. She started to pick up on who would spend a longer time in the interview process with Hawking. Those who walked in with a confident air seemed to fit the profile he was looking for, while the others, who were obnoxiously looking at themselves in the window reflections or flirting with her, left quickly. She completely approved.

When the interviews were finished, Hawking walked out of the conference room with his notes and a stack of applications, stretching as he returned to the desk. "I think we're going to be in good shape," he announced.

"I don't know anything about security, but the people you were actually considering fit were ones I would've concentrated on, too," Sadie shared.

"Great minds and all that," Hawking murmured. "I'm going to get Magnus to do some background checks on my choices and start calling people to offer them jobs."

Rocco

"I'll hold down the fort here," Sadie said cheerfully.

"Call before you need help," he said meaningfully.

"Of course," she answered. As he walked away, she buried herself in the task of scheduling the laundry and housekeeping staff training.

The rest of the day was quiet. Since the guys were handling the repair staff at the rear entrance, the lobby was deserted of everyone but her. It was almost eerie, but she soon got used to it as she made major strides through all the work that had piled up.

"Hey, Little girl." Rocco's voice broke the silence. "I brought lunch. Put a bookmark wherever you are and take a break."

Sadie jumped and looked up. "Wow! You need to clomp when you come down the hall. Aren't mountaineers supposed to wear hiking boots?"

"Not usually. For hiking, yes. Climbing mountains, no. Are you hungry?" he asked, tipping the tray her way.

"Starving. I was going to finish emailing and texting the new staff for training before I checked to see if the kitchen could send something over for me," Sadie shared.

"Mark your place and take a break now. If I know you, you've been putting off even going to the bathroom..."

"No, you said the B word!"

Immediately, Sadie walked as fast as she could toward the bathroom, squeezing her legs together as she chanted *no, no, no, no* in her mind. She'd studiously avoided thinking that word so she could get one more thing done before she allowed herself to go. She definitely should not have pushed it off quite this long. *Please don't let me have an accident!*

Pushing the door open, she ran inside, gathering her dress up from the bottom as she scurried to the first stall. *Oh, thank goodness!*

She couldn't keep her cheeks from flaming with heat as she exited the restroom to find Rocco lounging against the reception desk with their food still on a tray in his hands. "Sorry."

"That's not healthy, Little girl. You need to take a break without me being here to remind you."

"I know. I was so involved in what I was doing, I didn't think. Can we talk about something else, please?"

Rocco chuckled and answered, "Give me a kiss or two, and I'll forget everything."

"Deal!"

Sadie tried to lean over the tray but couldn't reach her Daddy, so she moved to the side and pushed the tray slightly out of the way to plant a good one on his lips. She was almost out of breath when she leaned away from him.

"That will do it," Rocco murmured. His gaze was fixed on her lips, and she knew what he was thinking.

"What's for lunch?" she asked to distract him.

"Some soup and sandwiches and a few mini cupcakes."

"Yum. I'm going to be sad when the kitchen stops experimenting with different dishes. I've loved everything," Sadie said as she led the way to a grouping of chairs in the lobby. "Shall we sit here?"

"This works great." Rocco put the tray on the table and uncovered the dishes, telling her what each one was. "Want to share or..."

"The broccoli cheese soup is mine. You can have the chicken noodle," she said, claiming the creamy soup.

"Or we'll both eat one," Rocco said with a grin as he watched her nab a spoon and take a bite.

"This is awesome. Try the other, and if you don't like it, I'll share," Sadie told him, crossing her fingers that he'd like the one she rejected.

Rocco

As she watched, Rocco tasted a spoonful of the soup and gave her a thumbs up. "You definitely missed out on this one. That's not canned broth—and those noodles are unmistakably homemade."

"Yum, I'm glad you like it," Sadie responded, not at all concerned that she had made the wrong choice. "I love cheese and broccoli. This is by far my favorite of all soups."

"Then this worked out exactly as it should," Rocco said, taking another bite of his soup.

The silence between them was comfortable and not awkward at all. Once her initial hunger was stated, she asked, "Anything going on that I should know about?"

"Kestrel replaced the broken cameras. We've got another order of them coming in so we can keep replacing them if we have to. He also hid a few in spots the bad guys won't look for. That should help us identify them more easily."

"Oh. That's good, I guess."

"Magnus hasn't seen anything suspicious today. It's been a quiet day all around. Some of the crews are finishing with the updates in the cabins. It looks like everything will be ready when the resort opens," Rocco assured her.

"That's great news. We're booked at half capacity when we open in three days, and then we'll launch fully after that," Sadie shared, knowing he had access to the same information that she did.

"Are you going to be ready?" Rocco asked.

"Sure. I'm positive we'll find more stuff we should've done before the opening, but we'll handle it. I like our team—you know, the seven of us and the staff we're gathering."

"Me, too. Would you like to come try your hand at mountain climbing? I'd love to have someone try out my beginner path."

"I don't know. I'm not really athletic," Sadie said, trying to wiggle out of his suggestion.

"You've never even thought about testing your problem-solving skills? It's really more about that than it is about brute strength—at least on the beginner path."

She sighed. "I am kinda trapped inside. I guess we could try it..." Sadie said, forcing herself to be brave.

"That's the spirit, Cookie. I'll even have the chef make us a gourmet picnic lunch to eat after we climb."

She grew less resistant to the idea now he'd mentioned food. It sounded like it would be more fun doing something other than just climbing. "You'll let me stop if I decide I'm not built for scaling the mountain face?" she asked.

"All you have to say is that's enough, and I'll get you down as fast as possible. There's no pressure here, Little girl. People either love it or hate it. Who knows? You might become my climbing buddy."

"That's never going to happen, but I'll try it with you. I like things that challenge me—at least once," she answered, hedging.

"We'll go tomorrow midmorning. It's supposed to be great weather, and we can enjoy some time together," Rocco announced.

She hadn't expected it to happen that quickly. "Maybe next week would be better," she muttered.

"We'll be in panic mode getting things done. You can take a couple of hours tomorrow for lunch and a climbing lesson, right?"

She pulled up her schedule, hoping that something would interfere, but there was nothing urgent. Taking a deep breath, she answered, "You'll make sure I'm safe, right?"

"Of course. As long as you listen to and follow my instructions, you'll be fine. Remember, I'm going to be taking a lot of people out for their first attempts when the resort opens."

"Right." She glanced over his chiseled physique. "I'm going to be scared."

"That's okay. It's fun to do things that push your limits every once in a while. It helps your brain stay active and alert."

"Oh, my brain will be alert. My body will hopefully be active and not frozen in fear," she joked.

"You can change your mind anytime, Sadie. You don't have to prove anything to me," Rocco reassured her.

"Thanks. I know that." She took a deep breath and added, "I really do want to try it."

"Perfect. It's a date," Rocco announced with a big grin that made him even more attractive.

"Thanks for bringing me lunch," she whispered.

"There's no one I'd rather spend time with, Cookie."

"I should get back to finishing things up if I'm going to take a couple hours off tomorrow."

Rocco shook his head. "You should go upstairs and take a power nap first."

She groaned. "I don't need a nap, Daddy."

He lifted a brow. "Is your bottom not sore enough from this morning, Sadie?"

She sighed. She wasn't going to win this battle. "How long do I have to rest?"

"How about thirty minutes. Set your alarm. I promise you'll be refreshed and more productive the rest of the day after you've had a nap."

"Fine," she grumbled as she stood.

Rocco stood also, cupped her face, and kissed her. "I trust you'll obey me without me following you to the apartment...?"

"Okay, Daddy," she murmured.

"Good girl. I'll meet you in our apartment before we go downstairs for dinner," Rocco told her.

"Oh, I could skip dinner." If she was going to nap, she should work later.

"Not happening. I'll see you at six," he said, his tone adamant.

"Yes, Daddy," she whispered, knowing he was right and her shift would be long finished by then. "Why are we going downstairs to eat?"

He winked at her. "That's going to be our usual dining location. The only reason we ate on the fifth floor yesterday was because you weren't yet aware of the basement's existence."

She was shocked. "Oh. Okay." They had eaten upstairs just to accommodate her? Wow.

"Give me a kiss, and I'll let you get back to all the important stuff you're working on."

Sadie leaned in to press her lips quickly against his and lingered as his arms wrapped around her to pull her body close. She relaxed against his hard form and responded eagerly to the magic that always happened in Rocco's arms.

"Six," he reminded her.

"I'll be there."

Chapter Twenty-One

She could get used to waking up in her Daddy's arms, Sadie decided when she found herself humming happily as she worked the next morning. All the men were amazing, but Rocco was special. She'd always dreamed of finding someone like him. The best thing was he seemed to feel the same way about her.

"Ready to go get changed, Sadie?" His voice made her jump in surprise.

"Is it time?" she asked, looking at her watch. Ten-thirty. She smiled at the handsome man, loving that he was obviously as eager to spend time with her as she was with him.

"It is. I put some clothes out on the bed in your playroom for you to wear."

Sadie hurried to gather all the things she was working on and rushed forward to wrap her arms around Rocco. "I won't take long!"

"Would you like help getting ready?" he asked with a twinkle in his eye.

"I can do it."

"That's probably wisest. I might get distracted."

Feeling her face heat, Sadie knew she was blushing. She liked it when he got distracted. His low chuckle told her he knew just where her thoughts had taken her.

"If you're sure you can get dressed without my expert help, I'll go pick up our lunch basket and get some water for us to take," he suggested.

"That's a very smart idea. I'll meet you here?" she said, running her hand over the reception desk.

"Ten minutes."

Turning, she walked as fast as she could in her short heels to the elevator. The elevator felt so slow but, finally, she and her impatiently tapping toes reached the top floor. After a press of her thumb against the entry pad, Sadie raced into Rocco's apartment and into her play space. She was grateful Magnus had recorded her thumbprint after the frightful night when she'd first learned about the basement. It was faster and easier, and her thumb was always with her.

When she entered the playroom, she smiled. There on the bed was a pair of flexible material shorts, a sports bra, and an official Danger Bluff *I climbed the Bluff* T-shirt. She laughed at the latter, knowing he'd raided the new supplies that were coming in every day to fill the gift shop. Stripping off her clothes, Sadie was surprised to find she was really looking forward to this. Time alone with her Daddy would be amazing—especially doing something that he loved so much.

She crossed her fingers as she stepped into her shorts. Hopefully, she'd be somewhat competent and enjoy the experience. She just didn't want to make a fool of herself.

Dressed, she sat down on the bed to pull on the socks and athletic shoes he'd left out for her. Rocco had assured her that she could start with her regular sneakers to try out the sport. If she liked it, he'd buy her gear that would help her tackle more challenging paths. Sadie had already decided the bunny path, or whatever rock climbers called the easiest one, would be hard enough.

In minutes, she was back at the desk to find Rocco waiting for her with a basket and a backpack of gear. "Ready! What can I carry?"

"I've got this, Cookie." Rocco easily shrugged into the pack and lifted the basket. He ushered her out the front door of the resort and into a waiting jeep.

"We'll save energy and ride to the cliff face."

"Okay."

Sadie hadn't been to this section of the resort. It wasn't far, and she enjoyed the beautiful landscaping the gardeners were in the process of restoring. "The guests are going to love this place. It's so gorgeous."

"Every day it gets better. I love seeing the improvements. I know you've been trapped inside getting everything ready there. We can take a longer tour when we're finished or do it another day if you would like."

"I'd love that."

Rocco parked at the bottom of the cliff overlooking the resort area. When Sadie lifted her hand to open the door, he wrapped his around her thigh to hold her in place. "Daddy's job is taking care of you."

"I can open my door, Rocco."

"I know you can, but it makes me happy to take care of you," he explained.

She smiled at him. He always made everything easier for her. "Okay. I'll wait."

"Thank you, Little girl."

Rocco slid out of the vehicle and circled around the front. She watched the magnetic man. He moved with the smoothness of a panther. His toned and muscled body fascinated her. Sadie couldn't wait to see his power in action as he climbed the cliff.

When he reached her side of the jeep, he stopped and looked all around the area before he opened her door. She tried not to think about the fact that he was being extra cautious about her safety.

There were still men somewhere who wanted to kidnap her. No need to harp on it constantly, but Sadie knew Magnus and the others were keeping a constant eye on the security cameras. Her Daddy would never take her out climbing like this if he thought it wouldn't be safe.

As he helped her out of the jeep, she stumbled a bit, too busy looking at the rock wall in front of her and not paying attention to the stones at her feet. Rocco stabilized her easily with an arm around her waist.

"I'm a bit of a klutz," she warned him.

"Everyone is when they try something new. Don't worry about looking good or being the best. Just be safe and have fun," he warned before patting her on the butt. "Come on, Cookie. Let's climb, and then we'll dive into the goodies the chef prepared for us."

"Lead on," she said with a smile.

In a few seconds, he had the equipment and their picnic basket unloaded. Rocco led the way to the beginning of the path he had created for the newest of rock climbers. Pointing at a low line of anchors he'd embedded in the rock face, he explained, "We'll try this one first to learn the process and gain confidence and then go a bit higher."

Quickly, he helped her into a harness and gloves and hooked her to the rigging he wore. "We're anchored together so if you lose your footing or grip, I can keep you safe."

"I don't want to pull you off the mountain," she protested.

"You won't. If you feel yourself slipping, give me some

notice. Don't worry if it happens suddenly and you can't warn me. I've got you, Sadie. I won't let anything happen to you. Remember, I'm trained to do this."

The look in his eyes guaranteed her that he'd never let her down. Sadie nodded and tried to relax. That tense feeling remained with her as Rocco led her onto the lowest path and helped her learn how to shift her grip and find toeholds. Each move felt easier, and she found herself enjoying the challenge.

When she jumped down the two feet to the ground at the end, Sadie threw herself into his arms. "I did it!"

Rocco twirled her around in a tight circle. "You not only did it, you were incredible."

"Incredible might be pushing it, but it wasn't as hard as I thought it would be," she confessed.

"Ready to try the next level?" he asked, pointing upward to the anchors ranging about seven feet from the ground instead of the two-foot-high path she'd just conquered.

"I can do it," she said confidently.

"That's my girl!"

After he coached her through the process of climbing up to the second level, Sadie looked down and, to her surprise, felt excited rather than scared to see the ground below her. She looked back at Rocco, who looked concerned. "I'm okay. I think I've decided this is fun," she said, laughing at herself.

"It is fun," he agreed. "Stay focused."

"Yes, Daddy," she said sarcastically, then swallowed hard at the reproving look he sent her. She was going to pay for that tone.

"Focus," he repeated, and she pushed that thought out of her mind.

Nodding, she pulled herself together. "I'm ready now."

"Good girl."

They were about halfway across the trail when she saw Rocco look over his shoulder. Glancing back herself, she saw a van approaching rapidly.

Rocco tapped his ear and frowned. "Damn! The battery must have died in my com. We're going to have to move quickly, Sadie. We don't want to get stuck here. There's a ledge ahead of us that's tucked behind some rocks. It will protect you."

She nodded and shifted her hands and feet as fast as she could as the van screeched to a halt and three men poured out. To her horror, she heard one man call out, "Kill them both."

A bullet chipped the rock off next to her head, and she froze. A strong hand grabbed her harness and yanked. Her body lurched to the side, swinging away from the rock face as Rocco hauled her around the rocks and onto a tiny ridge of rock that she would never have called a platform. Shivering in shock, she scrambled for a handhold to take the pressure of her weight off his body.

Clinging to the cliff, she whispered, "What are we going to do?"

"Did you put your panic button in your pocket?" he asked with his mouth against her ear as bullets pelted against the rocks.

"No. I'm with you. I didn't think I'd need it." Tears sprung to fill her eyes.

"It's okay, Sadie. I'm sure someone in the control center has seen the van. The guys will come to help us. In the meantime, we're going to stay in this protective niche but climb higher."

"Higher? Like to the top?" she asked, peering upward. It looked impossibly farther than she'd ever be able to climb.

"Concentrate on each move, Sadie. Don't think about

how far you have to climb. One hand and one foot shift at a time."

"I'll try." Sadie could already feel herself tiring. She was using muscles she was sure she'd never used before.

"I'll help you. It'll be okay, Sadie. I didn't just find you to lose you now."

She nodded, trying to be brave. "Just show me how."

"Team! A white van without license plates just plowed past me without stopping," Hawking's voice blared through the intercom.

Immediately, Magnus looked up at the screens to one side of him and located the vehicle as it sped through one zone after another. "I've got it, Hawking. Its trajectory seems to be the cliff face. Rocco and Sadie are rock climbing."

He sent out the location he expected they were headed to all the men as he tried to contact Rocco. There was no answer. "Rocco must not be wearing his earpiece," Magnus growled and tried calling. Rocco had obviously left his phone on the ground with his pack.

Locating each team member, he watched Hawking, Phoenix, and Caesar converge on the area around the van as Kestrel ran for the helicopter. "High alert. Major weaponry in front of you."

"Someone needs to remind them New Zealand has a ban against guns," Kestrel grumbled.

The brief silence that followed attested to the team's knowledge that the bad guys didn't follow the laws and would find a way to get what they wanted. "That sounded less stupid when I thought it," Kestrel muttered.

Magnus ignored Kestrel's statement and updated the team. "Rocco has Sadie tucked behind a jutting rock formation, and they're heading up. One of the bad guys has taken Rocco's spare harness from his pack, and he's heading up behind them. He'll have to climb up and shift over as well behind the rock barrier to shoot up toward them."

"We'll keep him from getting there," Phoenix promised. "I'm almost there."

"I'm pulling up in the air," Kestrel reported.

"Anyone armed?" Magnus asked.

"I'm there, Magnus," Phoenix said. "I don't have a gun, but I've got several knives. I'll shift to the right to pick off the guy on the bluff."

"Dammit. I only have a stunner," Hawking reported. "I'll work on taking out the guys on the ground."

"I brought the spearguns I was cleaning," Caesar reported.

"I've got you all on screen. Hawking, watch for Caesar coming from the right. Phoenix, you'll need to circle the van to get to the climber. Try to get close enough to slash a tire. Kestrel, cause a distraction in ten seconds," Magnus requested.

"On it," Kestrel answered, knowing that each team member counted with him as he ticked off the seconds before swooping down.

Magnus leaned forward, wishing he was there to help but knowing he was more valuable directing the team. He watched carefully, switching from the aerial view he could get from the copter to the security cameras placed in two trees.

Something crashed into the top of the van, making a dent. Magnus saw a flash of the Danger Bluff logo and recognized the smashed item as it bounced. Limited to what he could toss out of the window, Kestrel had dropped his metal water bottle.

"Good job," Magnus complimented him, knowing that Kestrel still heard him but was too busy to answer. He could see the men react and knew the impact had sent a reverberating sound through the area. Magnus had one last view of the men shooting upward before Kestrel zigzagged the copter out of range. That pass showed Magnus a glimpse of Phoenix slipping out of the shrubbery. They all relied on Phoenix to stab a knife into a tire and twist it to open the slit for the air to gush out.

In rapid succession, the cameras pointed toward the ground went black. The spray of bullets had taken out all his "eyes." Magnus slumped back in his chair. He could hear the spray of bullets and the exerted breath of the team. No one spoke aloud. His only view was of dots moving on the screen in front of him as the team shifted. It was up to the guys on the ground now.

Chapter Twenty-Two

"I don't think I can climb any higher, Rocco," Sadie admitted as she tried to rest against the stone wall.

"You've got this, Little girl. I'm right here with you."

Rocco moved lower, making her panic. "Don't leave me!"

"I'd never do that," he promised and shifted into position so her bottom rested on his shoulder.

Sadie could feel him taking some of her weight to ease the strain on her arms and legs. Not wanting to hurt him but too tired to boost herself off his support, she whispered, "Rocco, no!"

"I've got you, Little girl. There's a spot for us to rest above you."

She moved automatically as he steered her from below. Seeing the wider ledge to stand on, her energy flooded back, and she scrambled to safety. Rocco moved to shield her back and press her against the stone. The tips of her toes were still jammed into the rock crevasses of the bluff, but at least the ball of her foot now could support some of her weight. What in the world was Rocco standing on?

"Are you okay?" she whispered, flinching at the volley of bullets pelting around them.

"I'm stable, Little girl. I'm not going to let anything happen to you," he promised.

"How are we going to get away?" she asked, feeling shaky.

"The guys are below us. Kestrel is above. Can you hear the helicopter? One man is down already."

"How do you know?"

"The bullets have slowed."

Eager for any good signs, Sadie started counting the bullet strikes. She gasped as a shard of a rock splintered off next to them and flew directly toward her face. Rocco shifted sideways to put his shoulder in front of her, deflecting the threat. She felt him flinch.

"Did it get you? What can I do to help?" she asked.

"I'm fine, Sadie. A rock cut won't slow me down," he promised.

A sudden silence made them pause to listen.

A few seconds later, Phoenix's voice called to them. "Third man down. You're safe now."

Caesar's voice followed. "Want to go up or down?"

"Down," Sadie called immediately.

"We can either climb down, or if your arms are tired, we could repel," Rocco suggested.

"Repel?" Sadie's voice squeaked. "You mean like let go of the side of this rock and let the rope lower me?"

"Yes. Would you like to try that?"

"Not a chance," she responded without hesitation. The idea of letting go scared her to death. "Can we please climb down the way we came up?"

"Of course. We're going to do this together, Cookie. Just

like we got to this ledge. I'm going to move under you, and we'll ease our way down."

Without waiting for her to agree, Rocco crawled down the bluff until his shoulder again supported her. Slowly, they descended the rock face. Rocco coached her through the entire thing. She jumped when she heard a click and almost lost her footing. Rocco held her steady. Her heart raced as she clung to the stone.

"You're all right, Sadie. I should have warned you. I just clicked into the anchors for the second lowest track. You're almost there," Rocco soothed.

"We're that close?" she heard the tears in her voice and tried to compose herself.

"You've almost made it."

A few more supported shifts down and another click, and Sadie knew they were at the lowest level. "Hold on, Cookie. I'm going to lift you down," he said.

His supporting presence disappeared. Sadie clung desperately to the fingerholds in the bluff for the few seconds it took for him to step down on the ground. Rocco gripped her tightly around the waist and lifted her off the wall.

The minute her feet touched the ground, her knees buckled. He wrapped a strong arm around her and turned Sadie to face him. Pulling her close, he buried his face into her shoulder and simply held her. A second passed, and he moved back a fraction to look at her face.

Rocco lowered his lips to hers in a light kiss that expressed so much. His hands moved over her body. "Are you okay?"

"I'm good. But your shoulder! You're bleeding!" She yanked her hands out of her protective gloves to run her fingers down his arm. "You blocked me from getting hurt by putting yourself in danger."

"It's a scratch. I'll be fine."

"Promise?"

"Yes, Little girl. I promise."

"Rocco, the authorities are coming," Caesar warned. "Kestrel has called Kingsley."

"What happened to those guys? Why did they stop shooting?" Sadie fretted, trying to turn around to look.

Rocco simply scooped her up in his arms. "Tuck your face against my neck. You don't want to see this," he instructed and waited for her to obey. When she did so reluctantly, he carried her a short distance away and sat with her on the ground.

"We aren't going to say anything about your former boss, Sadie. We don't have any proof that it's him, and he's back in the States, so there's nothing they can do to him," Rocco said as he brushed her hair away from her face.

"What am I going to do? Kingsley isn't going to want me to stay here. I'm endangering everyone," she said, trying to hold herself together.

"We're going to take care of this, Sadie. Right now, we need to cooperate with the police while giving them as little information as possible. Can you do that for me?"

Sadie stared at his concerned face streaked with dust and sweat. Rocco had kept her safe while they'd clung to a cliff with their fingers and toes. He hadn't allowed her to panic and had supported her—literally. "I'll do what you say, Daddy."

"Thank you, Little girl."

"Here, Rocco. You both should drink these." Caesar appeared at their side with cold bottles of water.

"Thanks, Caesar," Sadie said, trying to keep her emotions from welling up too much but failing as tears tumbled from her eyes.

"It's okay, Little girl. We'll keep you safe."

"You did." Realizing what kind of danger they had dealt with, she asked, "Are you all okay?"

"I think Kestrel has a hangnail," Phoenix joked as he joined them.

"Where is he?" Sadie asked, looking up.

"He's back at the helipad. He'll bring the authorities here," Hawking said as he joined the group, holding a crushed Danger Bluff metal water bottle in his hand. "I found this. We may have to call him Hawkeye from now on instead of Kestrel. He dropped this bottle with perfect accuracy. That had to sound so loud when it hit the van."

"Kaboom," Caesar added, making an explosion gesture with his hands.

"They probably pissed their pants," Phoenix suggested as the sirens got louder.

Hawking glanced at his phone. "They're about a minute out. We'll walk through the scene with them since you guys were just hanging from the rocks, hiding from all the action."

"Did someone let Magnus know we're okay?" Rocco asked, looking at the massive men who stood in front of them.

"The rest of us have our earpieces in and can talk to him," Caesar ribbed Rocco. "Besides, that man knows everything, even when he's blind."

Rocco reached up to pluck the earpiece from his ear and held it up. "Battery's dead," Rocco said with a rueful shake of his head.

"Shit," Caesar responded. "Guess we better charge these every night. Maybe yours is faulty. Have Magnus take a look at it. They're brand new."

As the cars drove into the area, Phoenix, Caesar, and Hawking walked toward them to meet with the officials.

Rocco stayed with Sadie as the police interviewed everyone. Seeing Rocco's injury and how shaken up she was, the authorities had recommended they go to the hospital for treatment, but Rocco had assured them they had this level of medical treatment available at the resort and just wanted to get cleaned up and rest after their ordeal.

He answered a lot of the questions for them as Sadie claimed honestly that as a beginning rock climber her focus had centered on clinging to the bluff. There wasn't much information they could get from two people who had hidden throughout the skirmish other than who they were and why they were in New Zealand.

When the authorities transported the van and bodies away, Sadie's last bit of energy evaporated. Rocco led her to the jeep and tucked her into the passenger seat. After buckling her safely inside, he drove back to the main building.

"What am I going to do, Rocco?" Sadie asked as they pulled up in front of the resort. "I can't just stay here, but I sure don't want to be out in the world for them to find me when they come after me again."

"That's not happening, Little girl. You're staying close to us. Give the team time to handle this for you," Rocco told her gently before circling the car to help her out.

"The team? What are you guys? No one panicked. Everyone came running. How are six random resort employees on a team that handles bad guys with guns and a plan to kill a front desk manager? This is like out of a movie. Now on the big screen, you thought they were only the security guy, the scuba instructor, the IT expert, the climbing pro, the helicopter guide, and the maintenance supervisor, but they form The Team," she said, putting those last two words in capitals with the emphasis in her voice.

"You're tired, Sadie, and need a shower and food. Let's

take care of those things first before I answer all the questions bouncing around inside your head."

Those kind words destroyed the shaky supports Sadie had bolstered herself with to stay functional. He was right. All the bad guys were gone. If her old boss sent more people, it would take at least a couple of days for them to reach the resort. Her legs started shaking with the effort to stay upright.

"Come here, sweetheart. Let me take care of you."

Rocco swept her up in his arms and carried her through the building to the elevator and directly up to their apartment. Stripping off their dusty clothes, he led her into the shower and quickly washed the grime and sweat from her body before propping her up against his chest to wash her hair. His fingers scrubbed gently over her scalp, drawing a groan of appreciation from Sadie's throat. It felt so good.

When he finished pampering and cleaning her up, Rocco wrapped a towel around her damp hair and body before scooping Sadie back into his arms to carry her to his big bed and tuck her between the crisp sheets. Immediately, her eyes closed. Sadie felt his lips press against hers for a brief second before his presence moved away.

Rocco called down to the kitchen for soup and sandwiches. Sadie wasn't hungry even though she realized they hadn't eaten their picnic lunch. Her mind was too boggled to register if she needed fuel or not. From the muscle aches she felt already, Sadie knew she'd expended more energy than she had for a very long time. If she'd had to hold on one more second... She shook her head where it rested on the pillow.

"Are you okay, Cookie?" His warm hand stroked over her shoulder.

"I'm..." Her voice trailed away. "I don't know how I am. I do know I'm safe and clean. Those two things feel very good right now. Go finish your shower. I'll rest."

"I'll be quick."

When his footsteps faded away on the thick carpet, she listened carefully for the shower to turn back on. The quiet following the splashes of water told her when he'd finished cleaning up. She needed to keep track of him.

"Come here, Sadie," he said, helping her sit up in bed.

Rocco unwound the towel from her damp hair and carefully combed it out, taking his time not to yank her sensitive scalp. She loved all the soft kisses he pressed to her shoulders and neck. They made her feel precious and loved.

That last word echoed in her brain as her feelings gathered inside her. How could she be in love with a man she'd only known for a few days? Was it just because he'd saved her life, not just once but twice? Somehow, she knew it was more than that.

Sadie bit her lip to keep the words inside. He would simply think she was overwhelmed by what had happened today. She needed him to believe this wasn't just a reaction to being frightened by the threats to her life.

A knock on the door interrupted his care, followed by Caesar's voice calling, "Rocco, the kitchen just delivered food. I think we all ordered at the same time. Does Sadie feel like joining everyone in the common area?"

Rocco leaned to the side to see her face clearly. Sadie nodded eagerly. She needed to make sure they were okay as well. "We'll be there in a couple of minutes. Thanks, Caesar."

"I think there's a robe in my closet," Sadie pointed out.

"I've got it in here, Sadie. I'll grab both of ours."

In just a few minutes, she held Rocco's hand as he led her to the table. Sadie clutched the neck of her robe, realizing that she had to look awful—wet hair, no makeup, and naked under her robe. The sight of the men's concerned faces looking at her wiped all that away. Sadie flew around the table, hugging each one and thanking them for helping her. She stopped at Magnus's side when he held up a hand to hold her off.

"I wasn't even there."

"You were, too. Someone had to track everyone. You were juggling eggs over your head faster than everyone else." She wrapped her arms around his neck and hugged him close as she whispered, "Thank you."

"You're welcome, Little girl," Magnus said with resignation as he hugged her back.

Sadie couldn't keep from grinning as she looked around at all of them. "Of course, I had to end up with a posse of bad-ass Daddies."

The reality of that statement registered, and she swallowed hard. "What are we going to do about Mr. Pushkin?"

"We're going to take care of it," Rocco assured her.

"We can't endanger Mr. Kingsley's guests," Sadie said urgently. "I should just leave."

"That's not going to happen." Rocco put his foot down for the tenth time.

"Then what are we going to do?" she asked, repeating her earlier question.

"*You* aren't going to do anything except get the resort ready. We're going to handle it," Kestrel added.

"Okay? You'll keep me informed, right?"

"We'll tell you everything we can," Magnus said guardedly.

Sadie knew that was the best she could hope for. "Let's eat then. I know I'm starving."

The men echoed her statement, and the conversation focused on the food that filled the table before them. Sadie would visit the kitchen tomorrow to thank the employees for the delicious dishes they'd whipped up. She lifted the lid of the covered plate in front of her to find a steaming hot omelet and all the fixings. Her first bite made her eyes close. Apparently, sandwiches weren't the only thing the kitchen had sent up. There was a wide variety of comfort foods. She was one lucky Little girl.

Chapter Twenty-Three

"No! Get away!" Sadie yelled, punching the warm body that restrained her, her mind captured by the threat that menaced her in the dark.

"Ouch, Little girl. It's just me. You're safe here on the fifth floor with six bodyguards," a familiar, deep voice reassured her.

"Rocco? Daddy?" she corrected herself automatically.

"Yes, Cookie. I'm here."

"I had a scary dream. We were perched on the wall, and they climbed up after me. One grabbed my ankle and tried to shake me loose. I was so afraid I would fall."

"That is an awful nightmare, but it's your mind reacting to the attack today. You're safe here with me," he said and pressed a light kiss to her lips.

The desire to feel alive flared inside Sadie. She thrust her fingers through his thick hair and pulled his lips back to hers. Putting every bit of her desire into the deep kiss she pressed to his mouth, Sadie hoped he'd understand that she needed him.

Heat built between them. Rocco didn't ask any questions but simply responded avidly to her advances. His hands stroked over her skin and curves, making her feel beautiful, desirable, and loved. He pressed kisses here and there, tasting her skin. She loved his murmured sounds of enjoyment and appreciation.

"I need you," she whispered.

"I'm here, Little girl. I'm always going to protect you."

"Thank you," Sadie answered with genuine gratitude. She knew it was true and heartfelt.

"Let Daddy make you feel good," he murmured against her skin as he kissed across her aching shoulders, distracting her from the worst of the discomfort. He slipped a hand under her to massage the muscles across her upper back as he thrilled her with nips and caresses to her skin. She arched toward him when he rolled her nipple between his teeth.

Her eyes closed to focus on the sensations he lavished on her. His hand, cupping her breast, felt rough from the abrasions of the tough climb. She loved the slight scuff on her tender skin. It reminded her they were still alive and that this amazing man had kept her safe. Nothing else mattered but him.

He brushed rough fingertips down the center of her body. She knew he would find the slick wetness that gathered between her thighs. Spreading her legs eagerly, she welcomed his touch. A sigh of pleasure escaped from her lips as he explored her.

Those talented fingers tempted and tantalized as he pushed her arousal higher until she begged, "Please. Please. I need you inside me."

"That's exactly where I need to be, Sadie girl." He pressed two fingers deep inside her tight channel and wiggled them slightly as he slowly dragged them from her body, touching all those sensitive spots inside her that zinged with delight.

Sadie froze when his fingers didn't glide back inside her but trailed down to her smaller, puckered opening. Using the slick fluid that coated his fingertips, Rocco pushed two fingers through that tight ring of muscles. The faint taste of pain pushed her arousal higher as he delved into a place she'd always considered taboo.

"No, Daddy. Not there!" she protested.

"Let it feel good, sweetheart. I promise you'll enjoy having Daddy breach you here," he informed her gently.

"I've never..."

"I'll take care of you. We'll start stretching this tight bottom hole tomorrow. I have a perfect set of plugs to help you enjoy your Daddy being in this cute bottom."

She tried to pull her legs together, but he quickly shifted between them, anchoring her in place. *Don't respond! Don't respond! Don't respond!* Her efforts to show him that she didn't enjoy the forbidden invasion flopped horribly as her juices oozed from her body.

"It's okay to like my touch, Cookie. That's a good thing."

She nodded her head, unable to deny Rocco anything.

His low chuckle wafted over her, making her already beaded nipples clench even tighter. His fingers continued to move inside her as she wiggled and squirmed, not to get away but to help him build the sensations.

"There will be no place on your body that I will not touch, and I'll make sure you love every minute."

Her heart leaped in her chest, making her blurt out the truth she'd been hiding, "I love you, Daddy. I can't imagine a day without you."

"I love you, Sadie. More than life itself."

His fingers slid from her body, leaving relief and disappointment in their place. She couldn't imagine that he would target every part of her body for pleasure and that she would respond eagerly to his touch. Her eyes focused on his face. The desire blazing in his eyes told her just how much he enjoyed tantalizing her.

Shifting upward, he opened the drawer in the nightstand to pull out a small packet. In seconds, he'd slid a condom into place. Pressing the thick head of his cock to her pussy, he hesitated before pressing himself deep inside her slick opening. He rubbed his thick shaft against her as he filled her completely.

Once fully inside, Rocco ground the base of his cock against that small nerve bundle at the top of her channel. Sadie lifted her legs to wrap them around his hips, giving him full access to press farther inside. His groan of enjoyment made her smile. She tightened her muscles around him as he glided out.

"Temptress!" he growled and captured her mouth to share long kisses that made her want more.

When he ripped his lips from hers, she couldn't hold back her feelings anymore. "I love you!"

"I love you, too, Cookie. I'm never letting my Little girl go."

He withdrew and surged back into her, driving the breath from her lungs. She clung to him as they moved against each other. The sensations built deep in her abdomen. She needed to come.

"Daddy! Help me," she pleaded, feeling on edge and needing something more.

He slid a hand between her legs. That rock-roughened thumb brushed back and forth over her clit, giving Sadie the last push she needed to explode. He gentled his thrusts to extend her orgasm. When her fingers curled into the skin of his shoulders, Rocco repeated the process to build the tingles inside her back up to a critical point. He kept her there until she squirmed under him, begging him to let her come.

"Please, Daddy."

"Come with me, Sadie," he ordered before thrusting fully into her in long quick movements. His thick cock brushed rapidly over those sensitive spots as his touch stimulated her directly.

With a scream into the empty room, she felt herself clamp around his shaft as her orgasm overwhelmed her.

"Sadie!" he shouted a moment later as she felt warmth jet into the protective sheath.

Sweet kisses and whispered *I love yous* followed as he kept her close. Cuddled on his chest, Sadie wished she could stay in his arms forever. Yawning, she closed her eyes and dropped into a deep sleep.

Sadie stretched a hand out toward her Daddy and felt only cold sheets. Blinking her eyes open in confusion, she registered that the space was too quiet for him to be in the apartment. He must have gone to the common area, letting her sleep late.

She glanced at the time and panicked. It was way past time for her to be at the front desk. Launching herself out of bed, her heart responded to her panic and pounded in Sadie's chest. Every muscle in her body ached as she forced herself to move quickly.

"Ouch, ouch, ouch," she chanted as she ran into the closet on feet that felt like they had been jammed into tiny cracks in a bluff to support her weight.

Rocco

Snatching clothes willy-nilly from her hangers, Sadie found herself putting on the black pants and neon pink top. Too late to change, she stepped into the pumps on the closet floor, grabbed a comb and her phone, and ran toward the door, yelling, "Sorry, Daddy. I'm late."

Her chant resumed immediately as she stepped into the hallway and then the elevator. "Ouch, ouch, ouch!"

It wasn't until the door closed that she realized the common area had been completely abandoned. When the elevator reopened on the ground floor, she limped to her desk and waved her hands frantically in front of the security camera. Immediately, her cell rang. A name appeared on her phone that wasn't the one she wanted to see.

"What's wrong?" Magnus asked. His voice was steady as it always was. Nothing seemed to rattle or amuse him. The thought had popped into her mind days ago that he had hung around computers so long he'd become mechanical.

"Oh, thank goodness. You're there."

"Yes. I could better help the team from here than I could in the States."

"The team went to the States?" she asked, staring at the security camera as if she were staring at Magnus.

"Yes."

"Rocco left without telling me?"

"Check your phone, Sadie. He left a voice message for you."

"I'm all alone?"

"I'm here, Sadie. I'll make sure you're safe."

She shook her head. It wasn't the same. She knew Magnus would fight any adversary to keep her from danger, but... "I want my Daddy," she whispered.

"I know. It's going to be okay, Sadie. The team's going to take care of the problem that keeps following you. It's already

183

started. They're going to make sure it's finished this time before more men can be sent after you."

"Finished? Started? What are you talking about? They're not going after Sylvester Pushkin? That's suicide. He has all sorts of goons around him," she said in shock.

"Trust your Daddy. He'll come home to you and bring the rest of the team. Listen to your voicemail."

"And then what? Try to work while I worry that he's being killed?"

"I'd change your shoes first," Magnus suggested. His voice held the first hint of humor she'd ever heard from him.

"My shoes?" she repeated before looking down at her feet. She wore one blue pump and one red one. "Good heavens!"

"Take a few deep breaths. Listen to your message. And trust your Daddy and the team. They can take care of everything," Magnus suggested.

"I don't like this," she protested.

"I like the array of colors. You're wearing something to match just about any earrings you want to wear."

"Magnus! You are awful," she said, shaking her head. She couldn't keep herself from enjoying his dry sense of humor. "Can you at least show me where they are on the map?"

"The signal will be sporadic as they pass through the timelines. I'll send a link to your computer in the office."

"Thank you, Magnus."

Sadie disconnected the phone call and waved her thanks to the camera before retracing her steps to the elevator. She didn't have anyone scheduled for training or an hour-long interview. Just in case her Daddy was accessing a view of her through the cameras as Magnus had, she'd put herself together a bit more.

Rocco

She waited until she was alone in the apartment to listen to his message:

Cookie,

I need you to be brave for me. We know the threats against you will never end as long as that man is after you. The only solution is to make sure he is locked away or eliminated. Magnus will look after you. You can sleep in our bed or on the couch in the basement where Magnus hibernates.

Try not to worry. I know that will be hard to do, but I want you to try. Be good and stay where Magnus can monitor you. He won't let anything happen to you.

I love you, Sadie.

Ten minutes later, she wore a black-and-white tunic over her black pants and two matching black slip-ons. She pasted a determined smile on her face and went to work. There was a looming resort opening that she needed to prepare for even though key members of her staff were missing...along with her heart.

Chapter Twenty-Four

Waking up on the surprisingly-comfortable cot Magnus had set up for her in the shadows away from his computer, Sadie hugged all four penguins. She'd brought them down from her playroom and they were hogging her bed. She kissed each one as she greeted them. By this time, they'd all shared their names with her and were settled in happily with her childhood stuffie.

"Good morning, Edgar, Thomas, Peter, and Samuel." She had known the other penguins would have formal names to match the tuxedo worn by all of their species.

"Good morning, Sadie," Magnus called. He sounded as wide awake as he'd been last night when he'd ordered her to bed.

She tossed back the covers and ran toward him. "Any news?" she asked.

"Nothing new. Remember, the flights were long to get to your old home. Give them some time."

"It's hard to wait," she bemoaned.

"I know. There's oatmeal for breakfast," he said, pointing to a large insulated server and dishes.

She wrinkled her nose. "Oatmeal. That's not very exciting."

"But healthy for Little girls. The chef hid some brown sugar in the mix of extra additions."

"Oh. That's totally different then...."

She paused by his side, wanting but not wanting to ask a question.

"They're all fine, Little girl. No change in their biometrics."

"Biometrics?" she echoed.

"I can track their heart rate and a few other things. The team is fine. In fact, they got more sleep than I did last night."

Sadie waited to feel the stress ebb out of her shoulders. It didn't happen. Even knowing they were okay now didn't help her relax. She would be on edge until her Daddy held her in his arms.

"I guess I should go get dressed."

"Eat first, Little girl. Your Daddy will be angry if you don't take care of yourself," Magnus quietly reminded her.

"Okay. Can I leave my stuffies down here today?"

"I will watch over them," Magnus promised.

"Thank you."

Walking slowly to the waiting serving dishes, Sadie wrapped her arms around herself. *He needs to be okay. I need him home.*

Maybe she should spank him for making her worry. A giggle escaped her lips at that visual image popping into her brain. Not wanting to forget to tell her Daddy that, Sadie ran back over to grab her phone. She opened a new note and made a to-do list.

#1. Spank Daddy

Giggling again at the thought, she ladled the hot, creamy oatmeal into her bowl and added cranberries, brown sugar, walnuts, and cinnamon. Sadie sat at the table and took a bite. She looked around at all the empty seats and felt even more alone. To her surprise, Magnus stood and came over to help himself as well. He sat down to eat with her.

"Aren't you going to have brown sugar and all the yummies?" she asked.

"No, Little girl."

Silence filled the room as they ate. Finally, Sadie grabbed the oatmeal ladle and started talking about what she planned to work on that day. Holding it out to Magnus when she was done, she waited as long seconds passed by. To her delight, he took the ladle with a sigh.

"Whoever started this should be banned from the dinner table," he muttered. "Today, I'm going to keep track of five guys and watch over the resort to make sure everything continues on schedule. The grand opening is coming up."

Sadie reached out a finger to touch the ladle and asked, "What will you do when it opens?"

"I'll continue to gather intel down here and keep the system updated. Don't you need to be at the desk in a half hour?"

"Yes. I lost track of time." Sadie ate the last spoonful of food and stood. "Thanks for having breakfast with me," she added.

"I'll update you."

"Thanks, Magnus." Impulsively, she darted forward and hugged him.

"You're welcome, Little girl."

Rocco

By the third day, Sadie was getting grumpy. In her mind, she knew it was a long distance between the U.S. and New Zealand, but she wanted her Daddy home. Grabbing her phone, she added:

#2. Daddy needs to take me with him next time.

As she set the phone down, it rang, scaring her. Sadie juggled the phone and finally captured the tumbling device safely in her hands. Rocco. Frantically, she accepted the call.

"Daddy?"

"Hi, Cookie. I'm getting on the plane to come home. I'll be there in a few hours."

"Are you okay?"

"Yes. I miss you."

"I've missed you so much. You need to take me with you from now on," she demanded. "And I get to spank you."

"Whoa, Little girl. The only bottom that might need a spanking is yours for sassing your Daddy."

His stern tone sent a shiver down her spine. "Sorry. I've worried about you."

"I will climb mountains to get back to you, Little girl. I have the best incentive ever to return home safely."

"Is everyone else okay?"

"The whole team is loading up on a plane. We'll be home soon, Cookie. Be good. Tell Magnus to pull up the local news here."

She whispered goodbye and watched the screen go dark. A few seconds later, Sadie remembered what he'd said. After running to the elevator, she pressed her fingertips to the screen to access the basement.

Bursting from the car as the doors open, she called, "*Magnus!* They're coming home! Rocco says to pull up the U.S. news."

"On it," he responded as he typed furiously into the computer.

Finishing, he pointed to the display. "Watch that screen."

A news anchor she recognized spoke, "There was a raid today on the Pushkin Company. You can see the FBI carrying boxes of files and computers from the building. The business will remain closed indefinitely as the owner, Sylvester Pushkin, is being held without bond in a federal facility, awaiting his court date. The charges are serious and include allegations of tax fraud, sales of illegal goods, and racketeering. If convicted of all the crimes, Mr. Pushkin will be incarcerated for the rest of his life. A number of his employees also face numerous charges."

Magnus turned off the feed. "Looks like your Daddy has taken care of the problem. You're safe now."

"Do you think so?"

"Yes."

Feeling like she was walking on air, Sadie returned to her desk and forced herself to concentrate. The resort would open soon. She needed to be ready. An idea struck her, and she pulled out her phone.

#3. Make love to Daddy.

Warm arms wrapped around her, and Sadie cuddled against a familiar, muscular chest. She wrapped her arms around his neck as she blinked, trying to wake up. "Daddy?"

"I'm home, Little girl. How about if we sleep in our bed tonight? Want to grab Edgar and his buddies?"

"They should sleep down here, Daddy. It will be too noisy in our room for them to doze."

"Too noisy, huh?" Rocco asked, carrying her toward the elevator.

"Are you going to tell me what happened?" she asked.

"No. There are some things Little girls don't need to know. What's important is that you're safe. Give Daddy a kiss."

Thrilled to have him home, Sadie pressed her lips against his and poured all her feelings into the exchange. Her Daddy responded skillfully, making her squirm in his arms.

"The elevator is open." Magnus's amused voice reached them from the computer command center.

Without looking, Rocco walked inside. Sadie leaned back to select the fifth floor before returning to show her Daddy just how much she'd missed him. She watched out of the corner of her eye this time for the opening doors.

"Bed, Daddy."

"Your wish is my command, Cookie." Rocco strode toward their room but stopped to look at the door and set her feet on the carpet. "You colored all of these?" he asked in amazement as his gaze swept the walls.

"Me and the penguins. We had time to fill. Magnus isn't Mr. Chatty."

Rocco's laugh thrilled her. She hugged his waist, getting as close to him as possible. "Make love to me, Daddy," Sadie whispered. "I put it on my list, so it has to happen."

"The same list that contains a Daddy spanking and a demand that I always take you with me?" he asked.

"Yes. You've got to at least make one come true."

"I know what I'm choosing," he declared, leaning over to scoop her over his shoulder.

As he carried her inside, she dared to make the first one come true as well.

"You are in so much trouble, Little girl," he declared,

sitting on the bed and arranging her over his hard thighs. "Let's deal with this misbehavior first."

Sadie nodded eagerly as he pushed up her nightgown and tucked his fingers into her panties. "I've been bad, Daddy."

"Let's see if Daddy can make you feel good," he suggested as he dropped a heavy hand onto her bare bottom.

"Oh!"

Chapter Twenty-Five

Everyone sat around the table in the commons area in the basement with exhaustion etched into their faces. Thank goodness the arriving guests were all settled in their rooms. The whirlwind of activity had challenged all the new staff members, including Sadie and the team. Thank goodness all their preparations and training had supported the grand opening.

"The resort is booked fully for the next month," Sadie reported as she helped herself to the delicious pot roast and vegetables the chef had prepared for their dinner. "Oh, I forgot."

She rushed to her blazer hanging by the door and dug in the pockets. After retrieving a small package, she returned to the table and circled around the side to stop beside Hawking. "This came for you today."

Hawking accepted the package and opened it over the table. A flash drive with the swirling symbol they all recognized dropped to the wooden surface as he fished out a small piece of paper.

Hawking Winther, your marker has been called into effect. Here is your assignment. Protect Celeste Blanke. The encrypted drive contains all the background information I can provide you.

Baldwin Kingsley III

Authors' Note

We hope you're enjoying Danger Bluff! Each of the men you've met in this series will get their own happily ever after. Stay tuned for all six books coming soon!

Danger Bluff:
Rocco
Hawking
Kestrel
Magnus
Phoenix
Caesar

About Becca Jameson

Becca Jameson is a USA Today best-selling author of over 140 books. She is well-known for her Wolf Masters series, her Fight Club series, and her Surrender series. She currently lives in Houston, Texas, with her husband. Two grown kids pop in every once in a while too! She is loving this journey and has dabbled in a variety of genres, including paranormal, sports romance, military, reverse harem, dark romance, suspense, dystopian, and BDSM.

A total night owl, Becca writes late at night, sequestering herself in her office with a glass of red wine and a bar of dark chocolate, her fingers flying across the keyboard as her characters weave their own stories.

During the day--which never starts before ten in the morning!--she can be found walking, running errands, or reading in her favorite hammock chair!

...where Alphas dominate...

Becca's Newsletter Sign-up

Join my Facebook fan group, Becca's Bibliomaniacs, for the most up-to-date information, random excerpts while I work, giveaways, and fun release parties!

Facebook Fan Group:
Becca's Bibliomaniacs

Contact Becca:
www.beccajameson.com
beccajameson4@aol.com

facebook.com/becca.jameson.18

twitter.com/beccajameson

instagram.com/becca.jameson

bookbub.com/authors/becca-jameson

goodreads.com/beccajameson

amazon.com/author/beccajameson

Also by Becca Jameson

Danger Bluff:

Rocco

Hawking

Kestrel

Magnus

Phoenix

Caesar

Roses and Thorns:

Marigold

Oleander

Jasmine

Tulip

Daffodil

Lily

Bite of Pain Anthology: Gemma's Release

Shadowridge Guardians:

Steele by Pepper North

Kade by Kate Oliver

Atlas by Becca Jameson

Doc by Kate Oliver

Gabriel by Becca Jameson

Talon by Pepper North

Blossom Ridge:

Starting Over

Finding Peace

Building Trust

Feeling Brave

Embracing Joy

Accepting Love

Blossom Ridge Box Set One

Blossom Ridge Box Set Two

The Wanderers:

Sanctuary

Refuge

Harbor

Shelter

Hideout

Haven

The Wanderers Box Set One

The Wanderers Box Set Two

Surrender:

Raising Lucy

Teaching Abby

Leaving Roman

Choosing Kellen

Unchained by KaLyn Cooper

Protected by Becca Jameson

Liberated by KaLyn Cooper

Defended by Becca Jameson

Unrestrained by KaLyn Cooper

Delta Team Three (Special Forces: Operation Alpha):

Destiny's Delta

Canyon Springs:

Caleb's Mate

Hunter's Mate

Corked and Tapped:

Volume One: Friday Night

Volume Two: Company Party

Volume Three: The Holidays

Project DEEP:

Reviving Emily

Reviving Trish

Reviving Dade

Reviving Zeke

Reviving Graham

Reviving Bianca

Reviving Olivia

Project DEEP Box Set One

Project DEEP Box Set Two

Sculpt

Arcadian Bears:

Grizzly Mountain

Grizzly Beginning

Grizzly Secret

Grizzly Promise

Grizzly Survival

Grizzly Perfection

Arcadian Bears Box Set One

Arcadian Bears Box Set Two

Sleeper SEALs:

Saving Zola

Spring Training:

Catching Zia

Catching Lily

Catching Ava

Spring Training Box Set

The Underground series:

Force

Clinch

Guard

Submit

Thrust

Torque

The Underground Box Set One

The Underground Box Set Two

Wolf Masters series:

Kara's Wolves

Lindsey's Wolves

Jessica's Wolves

Alyssa's Wolves

Tessa's Wolf

Rebecca's Wolves

Melinda's Wolves

Laurie's Wolves

Amanda's Wolves

Sharon's Wolves

Wolf Masters Box Set One

Wolf Masters Box Set Two

Claiming Her series:

The Rules

The Game

The Prize

Claiming Her Box Set

Emergence series:

Bound to be Taken

Bound to be Tamed

Bound to be Tested

Bound to be Tempted

Emergence Box Set

The Fight Club series:

Come

Perv

Need

Hers

Want

Lust

The Fight Club Box Set One

The Fight Club Box Set Two

Wolf Gatherings series:

Tarnished

Dominated

Completed

Redeemed

Abandoned

Betrayed

Wolf Gatherings Box Set One

Wolf Gathering Box Set Two

Durham Wolves series:

Rescue in the Smokies

Fire in the Smokies

Freedom in the Smokies

Durham Wolves Box Set

Stand Alone Books:

Blind with Love

Guarding the Truth

Out of the Smoke

Abducting His Mate

Wolf Trinity

Frostbitten

A Princess for Cale/A Princess for Cain

Severed Dreams

Where Alphas Dominate

About Pepper North

Ever just gone for it? That's what *USA Today* Bestselling Author Pepper North did in 2017 when she posted a book for sale on Amazon without telling anyone. Thanks to her amazing fans, the support of the writing community, Mr. North, and a killer schedule, she has now written more than 80 books!

Enjoy contemporary, paranormal, dark, and erotic romances that are both sweet and steamy? Pepper will convert you into one of her loyal readers. What's coming in the future? A Daddypalooza!

Sign up for Pepper North's newsletter

Like Pepper North on Facebook

Join Pepper's Readers' Group for insider information and
giveaways!

Follow Pepper everywhere!
Amazon Author Page
BookBub
FaceBook
GoodReads
Instagram
TikToc
Twitter
YouTube
Visit Pepper's website for a current checklist of books!

amazon.com/author/pepper_north

bookbub.com/profile/pepper-north

facebook.com/AuthorPepperNorth

instagram.com/4peppernorth

pinterest.com/4peppernorth

twitter.com/@4peppernorth

Also By Pepper North

Don't miss future sweet and steamy Daddy stories by Pepper North? Subscribe to my newsletter!

Shadowridge Guardians

Combining the sizzling talents of bestselling authors Pepper North, Kate Oliver, and Becca Jameson, the Shadowridge Guardians are guaranteed to give you a thrill and leave you dreaming of your own throbbing motorcycle joyride.

Are you daring enough to ride with a club of rough, growly, commanding men? The protective Daddies of the Shadowridge Guardians Motorcycle Club will stop at nothing to ensure the safety and protection of everything that belongs to them: their Littles, their club, and their town. Throw in some sassy, naughty, mischievous women who won't hesitate to serve their fair share of attitude even in the face of looming danger, and this brand new MC Romance series is ready to ignite!

Available on Amazon

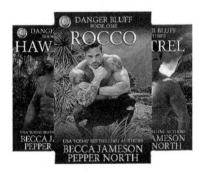

Danger Bluff

Welcome to Danger Bluff where a mysterious billionaire brings together a hand-selected team of men at an abandoned resort in New Zealand. They each owe him a marker. And they all have something in common—a dominant shared code to nurture and protect. They will repay their debts one by one, finding love along the way.

Available on Amazon

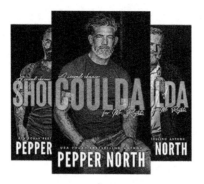

A Second Chance For Mr. Right

For some, there is a second chance at having Mr. Right. Coulda, Shoulda, Woulda explores a world of connections that can't exist... until they do. Forbidden love abounds when these Daddy Doms refuse to live with regret and claim the women who own their hearts.

Available on Amazon

Little Cakes

Welcome to Little Cakes, the bakery that plays Daddy matchmaker! Little Cakes is a sweet and satisfying series, but dare to taste only if you like delicious Daddies, luscious Littles, and guaranteed happily-ever-afters.

Available on Amazon

Dr. Richards' Littles®

A beloved age play series that features Littles who find their forever Daddies and Mommies. Dr. Richards guides and supports their efforts to keep their Littles happy and healthy.

Available on Amazon

Note: Zoey; Dr. Richards' Littles® 1 is available FREE on Pepper's website:

4PepperNorth.club

Dr. Richards' Littles®

is a registered trademark of

With A Wink Publishing, LLC.

SANCTUM

Pepper North introduces you to an age play community that is isolated from the surrounding world. Here Littles can be Little, and Daddies can care for their Littles and keep them protected from the outside world.

Available on Amazon

Soldier Daddies

What private mission are these elite soldiers undertaking? They're all searching for their perfect Little girl.

Available on Amazon

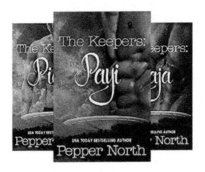

The Keepers

This series from Pepper North is a twist on contemporary age play romances. Here are the stories of humans cared for by specially selected Keepers of an alien race. These are science fiction novels that age play readers will love!

Available on Amazon

The Magic of Twelve

The Magic of Twelve features the stories of twelve women transported on their 22nd birthday to a new life as the droblin (cherished Little one) of a Sorcerer of Bairn. These magic wielders have waited a long time to take complete care of their droblin's needs. They will protect their precious one to their last drop of magic from a growing menace. Each novel is a complete story.

Available on Amazon

Printed in Great Britain
by Amazon

30097894R00126